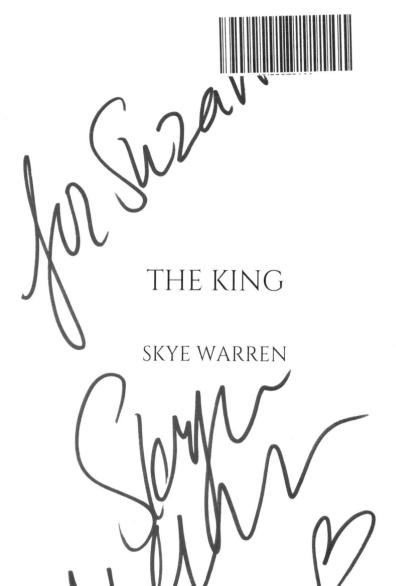

THE KING

SKYE WARREN

If you have already been introduced to this world by reading the prequel, THE PRINCE, you can skip to part two of this book.

If you haven't read THE PRINCE, or if you'd enjoy the refresher, turn the page to begin with part one.

Thank you so much for joining me with the new Masterpiece duet! Be sure to sign up for my VIP reader list where you'll get exclusive giveaways, free books, and new release alerts.

Part One

The Prince

CHAPTER ONE

ONE OF MAMA'S boyfriends took us on a trip when I turned four.

We visited this restaurant that had a special mermaid show. Metal bleachers lined up in front of a giant pool with see-through sides. Mermaids swam around in time to music while I watched with rapt attention.

Even though I could see the clear little tubes they used to breathe, even though I could tell the fins were made of fabric, it was magical to me.

I think I fell in love that day.

Inside the gift shop I found a stuffed blue-green mermaid with yarn hair and sparkly scales. I begged Mama to get it for me, but she said no. We never had much money.

The next day we went tubing in the river.

The tubes were black and slippery, the water dark. Not sparkly blue water like the mermaids had. I didn't like it but I knew better than to complain, especially with Mama laughing extra loud and Mama's boyfriend drinking beers from the floating cooler. He had what Mama called a *movie star smile*, but it just made him scary.

I held on to the tube as hard as I could, until my muscles were burning. It was too big for me to lay over the top, too big around even as I floated in the center, my arms slung over the large rubber sides. The river bumped me this way and that, taking me away from Mama until I pumped my legs to get back to her.

It happened suddenly.

The water got rough.

My hands slipped from the rubber.

I kicked hard against rocks smooth with algae. It hurt but I knew I couldn't stop.

The water sucked me down.

One minute I was floating in the middle of a big black tube. The next I was completely under, black currents swirling me around in circles, like a leaf in a hurricane. I remember the fear of it, the way I felt freezing inside, even colder than the water surrounding me.

The current slammed me to the bottom, the rocks hitting my back.

Then my head.

I don't remember what happened next, but someone must have pulled me out of the water.

Mama bought me the mermaid with green-blue hair to make me feel better. I kept that mermaid for a long time. Even after Mama was gone. I like to think it means she loved me, even if she ended up loving needles more. I found her in the bathtub one night, her grown-up things spilled over the cracked tile, her eyes open, her hands cold.

I didn't ever like swimming after that, even in sparkly blue pools.

After that I went to live with Daddy in the trailer park. I think he felt bad for what happened with Mama. He had this careful voice he used with me, like he thought I might cry. Even though I never did.

Daddy brought me to his parole meeting once. I sat in a chair with itchy fabric and wooden arms, trying not to look at the other men in the waiting room. The officer wore a brown suit, not a police uniform. He asked me if I liked living with Daddy.

"It's okay."

He leaned forward, his eyebrows pressed together. He had a big nose and a shiny head, but not in a bad way. It made me trust him. Like he was a regular person. I didn't trust people who looked too slick and handsome, the kind of men Mama dated.

The kind of men who bring needles as presents. The kind of men who disappear in the middle of the night with our rent money.

"Are you sure, Penny? You can tell me the truth."

I think he wanted me to tell him about the gambling, the nights we would go to the bar, when I would sit in the corner with a book while the men shouted and smoked and drank. The way Daddy would sometimes lose everything, even bus fare, and we would have to take the long walk back to the trailer park.

"I like it here," I tell him, because I do. There are no needles, and most of the time there's enough food. I can't trust that anything else would be better. "Daddy takes good care of me."

It was almost true when he brought me to his card games. The owner of the bar was named Big Joe, and he would usually give me a plate of French fries and a Sprite. Mostly I ate every day. That didn't last forever.

Once Daddy said I was old enough to stay home, it got worse.

He started staying out overnight, only coming back the next morning, his clothes rumpled and his eyes red. Then it was two days. Then three.

Four.

Now I watch the dirt road from the window, wondering if he'll come back tonight. I tried to make the box of mac and cheese last, but it's gone now. My tummy makes a loud sound. Daddy won't have much money, if he comes back now. He never does after the long trips. But I still keep wishing for him. Even if we were hungry, we would be together.

This is the longest he's been gone.

Worry presses down on my chest, making it hard to breathe. What happens if he doesn't come back? The same way Mama didn't come back? *No, don't think like that.* So I keep looking out the window, hoping I see his large form coming zig-zag down the lane.

When it gets to be nine o'clock, I take a bath and get into my favorite nightgown. I try to keep a regular bedtime even when Daddy's gone. It makes me feel like there's a grownup in the trailer.

I climb into bed, staring through the blinds on my window.

My bedroom faces the back of the trailer park, away from the city lights. I can see a line of dark trees that move in the wind.

Then a flicker of something. A light. A fire?

My heart pounds harder. I can feel it thump in my chest. Darkness creeps up in my mind.

What if Daddy's out there? What if he couldn't find his way home? He knows the way, but if he's been drinking a lot he might have gotten lost.

He's never been gone this long. That must be him.

I want it to be him.

I don't know whether the ache in my heart is hope or fear. *Both.*

Mostly I know better than to go outside after dark. Even if someone bangs on the door, the lock stays turned. Unless it's a policeman with a badge. But I'm too awake to fall asleep.

Then there's another flash of something bright through the trees.

I open the door slow, as if something in the shadows might jump at me. There's nothing, only the soft whisper of grass in the wind. No one mows around here. Weeds come up to my knees. Brambles poke the bottoms of my feet. I press through the trees, determined to find out what's on the other side.

There's a watering hole around here some-where. I've never been there. Never wanted to. But I've heard some of the kids on the bus talk about fishing there, before they moved up to middle school. I don't think they really meant fishing anyway, not with the sweet smoke floating through the brush.

The air sounds different as I reach the water. More of a gentle hum. Less rustling of leaves. I peek over a bush to see a wide black lake. It's bigger than I would have thought. The moon draws a long oval across the surface.

Then I see him.

A man sitting on the ground, his elbows resting on his legs. He's watching the water like it's got the answers he's looking for. Like there are mermaids inside.

Something stings my leg. An ant? I jump, bumping into the bush.

The sound breaks the silence.

He stands and faces me, moonlight across his face. He's younger than I thought. Maybe in high school. I think through the families who live in the trailer park, but no one has a kid his age. And I would remember him if I had seen him. There's something about the way he holds himself. Smooth and strong, so different from the hunched over way people move around here.

He's got something in his hand. It glints in the dark. Some kind of weapon.

"Who's there?" he says.

He doesn't sound afraid. *I don't want to be afraid.*

But I am. I take a step back, breaking a branch.

"Come out where I can see you! I have a gun. I'll start shooting if I have to."

Shooting? Part of me wants to run the other way, to keep running until I make it back to the trailer and lock the door. But what if he does start shooting? I take a step forward.

Then another.

I'm standing in front of the trees, trembling too hard to speak. He's maybe a few yards away, but it might as well be a few inches. Too close for me to run.

"Where's your daddy?" he says, like maybe he knows him.

I lift my shoulder. "Dunno."

"You alone?"

That's a scary question for a boy to ask a girl. "Are you?"

He lowers his weapon. "No one comes here. There's nothing but bugs and dirt. And maybe wolves."

Wolves? No one told me about wolves. "For real?"

"Haven't seen one, but I have a knife. I can fight if I have to."

"You don't shoot them?"

He looks away, like he's embarrassed. "That was a lie."

I understand that. And it means he *was* scared, even if he didn't sound like it. I understand that, too. I take a step closer to him, curious now. "Why are you here then? If there's nothing but bugs and dirt?"

"Better than home. Why are you here?"

Because I'm hungry. Because I'm lonely and afraid. The lake glistens dark, looking more like ink than water. "You ever go swimming?"

"Sometimes."

He's probably not afraid of the water. "Are there sharks?"

"Sharks don't live in lakes."

Bending down I touch the surface and find it cold. "What's here then?"

"Alligators, probably."

I pull my hand back. "You fight those too?"

"Nah, they have to be pretty desperate to go after a person. Mostly they eat fish."

Alligators don't sound like fun, whether they're desperate or not. Wiping my hand on my nightgown, I move away from the water. There's a little space with no weeds coming up. Only dirt. A sleeping bag and some food. Clothes spread out like they're drying. How long has he been here?

I glance at him. "You live here."

He lifts his chin. "And you live in the trailer park."

The way he talks to me, it's like I'm his equal. A person.

Most people dismiss me as soon as they look at me. I know I'm small, maybe smaller than other girls my age. Even Mrs. Keller looks at me different, like I'm special.

This boy talks to me rough, like he knows I can take it. There are twigs on the ground. When I pick one up I realize it's a reed from the water, dried out and snapped.

I press the sharp tip to the dirt and draw one side of a heart. Then the other.

"Go home," he says.

When I'm alone it feels like I'm on the moon, far away from anyone who can help, from anyone who would want to. "Daddy didn't come back. He went drinking."

"Does he usually do that?"

All the time. "But I ran out of food."

"I don't have any food," he says.

I shrug, because that's not why I'm out here. Not now. Something worse than hunger has been hounding me since Daddy left. The fear that he won't come back. *Like Mama.*

My stomach feels so high it's almost in my throat.

"It's okay," I say, the same way I told the parole officer. The same way the boy told me he had a gun. It's a lie we tell to make ourselves feel better.

He studies me, his dark eyes narrow. "What's your name?"

"Penny. What's yours?"

"Quarter," he says, his face completely serious.

It's such a grown-up joke. I make a face. "What do you eat then?"

"Fish, sometimes. If I can catch them."

He's living on fish? Then he's probably hungrier than me. "Like the alligators?"

"Pretty much."

It would be nice to catch fish, if I knew how. If I wasn't so afraid of water. If I didn't dream about slipping under. "Did your daddy teach you how to fish?"

"No. I don't have a pole or anything."

"Then how do you catch them?"

He doesn't answer for a long time. I almost think he's done talking to me. Then he says, "How long can you hold your breath?"

The question makes me shiver.

"Dunno." I've never stayed in water long

enough to find out.

"Most people can hold it for two minutes. Then carbon dioxide builds up in your blood. Your eyes get dark. And then you take in a breath full of water."

My eyes widen. *Black water. Sharp rocks.* "You're talking about drowning."

"I don't drown. Not for five minutes. Not for ten."

I suck in a breath, part surprise and part awe. He's like a wild animal. A tiger. Or maybe that black panther from the Jungle Book. Some people would think he's strange, but it's really normal people who are dangerous. With their needles and their *movie star smiles.*

He doesn't seem to realize how special he is, though. He looks almost sad about it. "Fish don't expect that, a person being so still. And when they're going by me, I stab one with my knife."

I can't even imagine getting into the water, much less putting my head under. And staying there. He really isn't afraid of anything. Not like me. "For real?"

He shrugs. "It's weird."

"I wish I could do that," I say, my throat tight around the words.

"Well, sure," he says, his voice sharp. "It's on

every little girl's to-do list. Learn ballet. See the Eiffel tower. Stab a fish with a knife."

"I wouldn't have to wait for Daddy to come home for food."

He looks away. "The whole camping outdoorsy trend isn't all it's cracked up to be. There aren't any pillows, for one thing."

That sleeping bag can't be comfortable on dirt. Why does he live out here instead of in a trailer? Why would anyone choose rocks over carpet? "Your daddy never came back home, too?"

"Oh, he's still there. That's the problem."

My heart squeezes. It's bad to want your daddy to come home, worse to wish he wouldn't. Whatever happened to this boy must be truly scary. "How long have you been here?"

"Maybe six months."

Six months is a long time.

The solution seems simple. I'm afraid to be alone in the trailer without a grownup. He's *almost* a grownup. "You can stay with me," I tell him. "I've got a pillow."

"No."

It means he wants me to leave, how short and sharp he said it. Something keeps my feet stuck on the ground. The empty trailer doesn't feel safe anymore.

This wild boy could protect me, with his knife and his courage.

"Can I sleep here tonight? I won't get in the way."

He studies me for a long moment. "Get in the sleeping bag."

Only then do I remember that some men do bad things to girls. "Why?"

"To sleep," he says, his voice mean. "What would I want with a puny kid?"

That's a good answer. I climb into the sleeping bag. It's not as soft or as warm as my bed at home, but it feels so much better. Like I'm safe here, even if I don't know his name.

Like I can breathe again, even though I'm so close to the water.

"I'll see if I can catch something," he says, "but the fish aren't active at night. And it's harder to see. Pitch black. I have to go by feel."

He can do that? And it's even more surprising that he *would* do that for me. It must be freezing in there. Why would he help me? No one else does.

I want to ask him why he talks to me like I'm somebody.

I want to ask him why he cares.

Instead I say, "Thank you."

Only when he ducks his head under do I see the green corner peeking out from inside his backpack. Money. I know enough about gambling to know that Daddy will come back empty handed. That means there won't be food, not for days. Or money for the gas bill. Or the lot rent.

And I know enough about gambling to know that I don't have a choice. You have to play the cards you're dealt. I reach out and grab it, crushing the soft bill in my hand. Then I turn toward the tree line and run.

CHAPTER TWO

THE GROUND IS soft beneath my feet, like it's made from Play-Doh instead of dirt. Rainwater pools beneath the seat of the swing, where years of feet have dug a hollow. Droplets cling to the steel bars, shaking from some unseen force.

Usually I'm on that swing, rain or shine. I kick my legs as hard as I can, until I'm flying. My hair covers my face. Tears sting my eyes. The playground becomes a blur.

When I get to the highest point, I think about letting go. Every time, back and forth. I imagine letting go of the squeaky chains that leave the smell of rust on my hands. In my head I don't crash to the ground. I keep going up and up, into the clouds.

Not today.

I was almost afraid to look at the money once I made it to my trailer, my heart pounding against my ribs. Like it could bite me if I smoothed it out. And when I did look I gasped. A hundred dollars.

Enough money to feed me for a month. Two months. Forever.

What is he doing living on the ground, fishing for food, if he has a hundred dollars? I thought it was a five-dollar bill. Maybe twenty at the most. He could have stayed at a motel in the west side for weeks with that money. Has he been gone from home longer than that?

It didn't feel right leaving that much money in the trailer, so I kept it in my pocket.

Maybe it weighs a hundred pounds too, because I don't feel like I can swing today.

Mrs. Keller has been acting strange since this morning. She keeps looking at the door, at the clock. When we go to recess she holds me back. "There's someone coming to see you."

All I can think about is the money in my pocket. He must have told someone. I'll be in trouble. My throat feels so tight I can't even speak. I stole something. *I deserve to be punished.*

"Don't worry," she says, smiling gently. "It's not bad. I told the principal how good you are in math. How you really need more than we can offer you. She got in touch with someone who can help."

So it's not about the money.

That doesn't really make me feel better.

I wander away from the swings and the slide. Away from the strange climbing gym that no one ever uses, its metal surfaces too hot or too cold. Patchy grass gives way to uneven dirt near the red brick wall. There's a place tucked into the corner, hidden from the street and from the basketball court where the teacher stands. A hiding place, but one I mostly stay away from. It's too easy to get trapped back here. Fifth grade boys are the worst. If they trapped me here, what would I do? Fight? Scream? I'm not even sure anyone would come.

I'm afraid to find out.

I hope the wild boy never trapped any girls here. Never pushed them. I don't think he would do that. He tried to help me. *And you stole his money.*

It smells bad in the hiding place, like mold and pee and something kind of sweet.

No one's in the hiding place today. That shouldn't make me nervous. Someone doesn't get beaten bloody every single day. Only most. A knot tightens in my stomach. I can't stand being out in the playground today, being around running and laughter.

A shadow appears over mine, longer and wider.

I turn around fast, but the sun blinds my eyes. There's someone standing there, way too close. How did he get here without me hearing him? I know it isn't Mrs. Keller. He doesn't have her curly hair or her dress. It's not Mr. Willis with his tennis shoes and track pants. This man's wearing dress shoes. An overcoat. And the way he stands, so tall and proud. So still. I know I would remember it if I'd seen him before, even without seeing his face. He looks strangely familiar. Like I know him from a dream.

"Hello, little girl," he says, his voice smooth like paint, spilling over my hands and turning them every color, mixing together until they're only black.

Is he here about Daddy?

I know my eyes are wide, hands tucked behind my back. "Hello."

"What's your name?"

The way he asks, I can tell he already knows. "Penny."

"Do you know my name?"

My stomach turns over. I shake my head, lips pressed together.

"I'm Jonathan Scott. Have you heard of me?" He doesn't wait to hear the answer. He probably knows that everyone's heard of him, even me.

Almost everyone in the city owes him something. "Mrs. Keller says you like numbers."

I don't like numbers. Not any more than I like breathing or sleeping. It's something I can do without thinking. It just happens. "I guess."

"She said you can do all kinds of tricks. Do you want to show me?"

Tricks. Like I'm a dog. And I never want to show anyone.

I don't want to show him in particular.

I have the sudden flash of Lisa Blake from two trailers down. Her family had less than us, which was saying something. They got in deep with Jonathan Scott. Then one day her momma got her a bunch of makeup from the drugstore. A new dress. She looked like some kind of beauty queen that afternoon. It was summer. And that was the last day I ever saw her.

The cops came around, asking questions, but everyone knew not to say anything. She just disappeared. No one mentioned the makeup. The dress.

Even the kids understood—we didn't want to end up like Lisa Blake.

"Okay," I say, my mind racing. I can't let him think I'm special. "I'm real smart," I add, with a touch of boasting, because I'd never really say that. It's pretend.

I don't want to be noticed by him, not for my brain and not for my body.

"Are you?" He sounds like I said a joke. "What's twenty-seven times forty-three?"

I pretend to think about it. "One thousand one hundred and sixty-one."

"That's right, Penny. And what about..." Now he's the one pretending to think. "What's sixty-nine times four hundred and twenty-eight?" After a moment he adds, "Point two."

I don't want to know the answer. I try to forget, but the number 29545.8 hovers in my mind. It's like he asked me my own name. I can't forget it if I try. "Can you say it again?"

He repeats himself, slow and patient.

I bite my lip, trying to look worried. "We haven't done points yet."

"Without it, then."

I worry the hem of my dress between my fingers, wondering where Mrs. Keller is. Why doesn't she come and help me? I know the answer. She sent him here. That's how he knew I liked numbers. This is who she was waiting for all morning. I was afraid of a group of small boys, when instead I only needed to worry about one big one.

"Twenty-nine thousand," I say, before taking a breath. "Two hundred and twelve?"

My failure hangs in the air, as thick as the leftover rain. I don't want to play it dumb completely. He would wonder why Mrs. Keller called him at all. It might get her in trouble. And worse than that, he might know I'm pretending.

"Or maybe twenty-nine hundred, five hundred…and forty-five."

"Correct," he says softly, but he isn't impressed. Not now that I've gotten it wrong.

I don't want to put red lipstick on. I don't want to wear a new dress. I don't want to be interesting to a man like this. He might want me for a different purpose than Lisa, but I'm safer if he doesn't want me at all. "Do you want to try fractions?" I offer him. "We started those."

"No, little girl. We're done here."

He turns and walks away, leaving me leaning against the red brick. Only when he's gone do I take a breath, that sickly sweet air a familiar relief in my lungs. For the rest of the school day I have to keep reminding myself that I can breathe. I'm not underwater.

Even if it feels like that.

✧　✧　✧

WHEN THE SCHOOL bus screeches to a stop in the road, a cloud of dust rises into the air, turned golden by the waning sun. The Happy Hills Trailer Park is to the west of the city, nestled between Tanglewood's slums and a ridge of wilderness on the other side. It gets dark here before anywhere else, in the shadows of either side.

My backpack feels heavy with the book Mrs. Keller gave me. *Trigonometry Proofs,* it says in large block letters. The cover is wrinkled and torn, the inside pages marked up with pencil. I don't know where she got it from, but she said it's mine now.

I want to go home and look inside, but there's a hurt inside that stops me. I don't think it's only hunger. Guilt. That's what I've been feeling all day, the hundred-dollar bill I stole burning hotter in my pocket with every minute of the day.

What I should do is return the whole thing, but it's already Friday. The school gives me breakfast and lunch with my number, but that leaves me awful hungry on the weekend.

The bus lurches forward, leaving me in the middle of the road. Dust settles back around me, a thin layer sticking to the sweat on my skin.

Instead of taking the path into the park I

follow the road to the end.

Thick burglary bars cover the windows of the Tanglewood General Store. Colorful lottery posters and cigarette ads peek through the black iron. A bell rings above me when I open the door.

Mr. Romero stands up and comes around the counter, leaving his baseball game playing on the small TV on the counter.

"Penny," he says, his voice scratchy. Nothing like the smooth voice of the stranger at school.

"Hello," I say without meeting his eyes.

If Daddy comes back with money I can get candy sometimes. Kit Kats are my favorite because I can eat one and save the rest for later.

Instead I head down the pantry aisle, where the noodles and peanut butter are.

I don't know if Mr. Romero thinks I'm going to steal something, but I've only done that a few times. He follows me down the row, staying too close for comfort. I pick a few cans of soup—mushroom barley and turkey rice. When I have four cans my arms are full. I walk to the counter and set them down so I can take out the hundred-dollar bill.

The bushy eyebrows on Mr. Romero's face go up. "Where'd you get that?"

I shrug, because he doesn't really want to

know. He doesn't really care.

"Your daddy come back?"

"Not yet."

A grunt. "He's been gone a long time, this time around. What's it been? A week now?"

Two weeks. "I don't know."

Mr. Romero runs a blackened rag across his forehead. "Runs off and leaves you behind. I know times have changed, but that doesn't seem right. I don't say anything to him usually, since he's one of my best customers."

Half the trailers in Happy Hills are empty. Some of them have squatters, but they don't spend much at the store. I'm sure Daddy has bought most of the lottery tickets that get sold here. Every so often he wins a hundred dollars, but it's never more than he spent.

There's such a long pause that I think Mr. Romero isn't going to sell me the soup. Then I would have to walk a long way into town to buy something else. Or most likely go hungry again.

"If your daddy doesn't come back, you come see me. You know which trailer I'm in."

There's a lot I'll do to survive—lie and steal. But I won't ever step foot into Mr. Romero's trailer. He looks at me like he's calculating. Not numbers, though. Something else.

If I went inside I don't think I'd ever leave. "Okay."

He presses a button and the register pops open. Slowly he counts out change.

Ninety-eight fifty-two. That's what I should get back.

He puts four twenty-dollar bills on the counter. A five. Two ones. Twenty-five cents.

It's short, so I hold my ground until he adds the rest of the money. Finally I meet his eyes. His flash with dislike. I don't like letting people see what I know, but it's not worth losing money over.

Especially when the money isn't mine.

He gives me a thin plastic bag, the handles stretching under the weight of the cans. I pass my trailer and head into the woods, the same way I went the night before. I have this idea for a deal. Or maybe it's a plea. Whatever the word, I'm going to offer the cans and the money back to the boy. Then he'll have what he started with, so maybe he won't be so mad.

Maybe he'll let me take one of the cans.

When I get to the lake there's no one there. Nothing left of his backpack or the Styrofoam or his grown-up magazines. Only a few scuff marks by the water to show that anyone was ever there at all.

CHAPTER THREE

THE FIRST TIME I cheat is by accident.
Most nights Daddy plays at The Cellar, a bar underneath an old hotel, the wooden wine racks still standing. In the back corner there's a table covered with fraying green fabric, its surface marked with burns and sticky blackness from a lifetime of games. The chairs around the table don't match—some of them stained cloth, others brown leather with stuffing poked out.

The chair I like best is cream-colored with drawings in blue—a boy chasing a puppy, a pie on a picnic table. It's like someone's happy childhood, wholesome and innocent.

On that particular night we get there early enough that the chair I want is empty. I tuck my feet underneath me and read a book, pressing my face into the pages, blocking out the voices and the smoke.

I'm deep in the world of fairies and dragons when I hear the clatter of poker chips. Out of the corner of my eye, I see Daddy tense up as he shoves most of his small stack into the center of the table.

I count up the colors. One hundred and fifty dollars in red, white, black, and blue.

My chest feels tight when I think about him losing that money. I'm so tired of being hungry. So tired of being scared.

From over his shoulder I can see his cards. A seven of hearts and a three of clubs. What could he be making with those? The other man left in the game has an ace and a jack of spades on the table. That could easily be a straight or a flush. Maybe even a straight flush.

Maybe even a royal flush.

It's wild to even bid against that. Daddy gets more reckless as the night rolls on, as the glasses of whiskey drain away. It's a sign that he's not completely drunk, that he's kept something back for the bus fare.

Even so, that's a lot of money in the pot.

He lifts the corner of his new cards. A single pair.

It's not very strong, and when the man across from us raises the bet, I can see that Daddy's ready to fold. It could buy so much food. And it's all we have left. The pot in the center? Almost a thousand dollars in clay. We could eat for weeks.

Months.

If he wins.

I tug on Daddy's arm. He mumbles something, not paying attention. None of the other men pay me any attention. Maybe they think I want money for the soda machine.

My heart squeezes.

"He doesn't have it," I whisper in Daddy's ear.

Most of the spades have been played in previous games. The only ones in this hand are the nine and six. Those are in the hands that folded. A straight is more possible. There are a lot of cards that can make that happen underneath, but the odds are with us.

And anyone would use such a strong initial showing to bluff.

He pauses, his hand clenched around the last chip.

We'll be walking home if I'm wrong about this. I might be no better than him.

Daddy throws the chip into the pot.

I can see the flicker of anger in the other man's eyes. Sweet relief lets me breathe again. The cards flip over, revealing a hand with absolutely nothing—the perfect bluff.

Our pair of sevens wins the largest pot Daddy's brought home in ages.

The good thing about that night is that I could make deals with Daddy after that. *I'll only help you win if you leave money for the gas bill.* The bad thing is it only encouraged him to play deeper and harder, losing himself in the game.

We came up with signals that I would use during the game, never leaving my seat so that no one would suspect. There are higher stakes games that I'm not allowed into, being a kid. Daddy loses more money there. He enjoys them more. That always seemed strange to me.

It's almost like he likes to lose, the same way that Mama did.

Is he going to leave the way she did?

That was before I met the wild boy by the lake.

Before I wondered if I share the same weakness, because I'm sitting in the trailer with almost a hundred dollars that isn't mine. That boy doesn't know which trailer I'm in but it would be easy enough to ask around and find out which trailer has a little girl. Daddy isn't even here to protect me. I told him that, didn't I?

"And you're supposed to be smart," I say under my breath.

What would my life be like if I hadn't told

Daddy about counting cards? Or if my brain were different, if I couldn't count them so easy?

I put the money under my pillow. It's not like I can spend it right now anyway. Leaving the trailer at night is a bad idea, especially with a strong boy who has a right to be angry with me roaming around.

If I had only stayed there I might have eaten last night.

I could eat right now if I open a can of soup.

Instead I pull out the heavy volume of *Trigonometry Proofs*. I feel bad for pretending to be dumb when the man asked me questions, especially after Mrs. Keller went through so much trouble. I know I'm supposed to trust grownups, but I don't trust him.

I lose myself in Pythagorean identities and inverse trig functions.

This is where things make sense. There's no such thing as hunger when I'm solving proofs, no such thing as darkness. No way to fall into the water while turning pages and twisting equations in my head.

WHEN I WAKE up the moon peeks between the plastic slats at my window, the quiet creak of the trailer the only sound. But I know something's different. The air feels different.

Someone is here.

My chest feels full with relief and a stupid kind of happiness, before I realize it can't be Daddy. He would never be so quiet, especially coming from a two-week bender. He would crash into the counters, bang his head on the door-frame, and swear in loud whispers before finally falling asleep with snores that rattle the walls.

A burglar? We don't have much of anything to steal, but people get dumb when they're desperate. Maybe Mr. Romero told someone I had a hundred dollars.

Or maybe it's Mr. Romero himself, come to my trailer since I won't come to his. My heart beats wild and loud, banging against my ribs like it's trying to break out.

"Trigonometry," says a voice in the darkness.

For a half second I think it's the man from school. The one who's tall and dark, his voice too smooth and his smile too cold to be trusted. Jonathan Scott. The terror that rises up in me is bigger and sharper than when I thought it was a burglar, or even Mr. Romero in my trailer. The very worst threat. The same as drowning, my very own nightmare.

THE PRINCE

And then my sleepy mind registers something about the voice. It's not deep.

"What's a little kid doing with a trigonometry book?"

I sit up in bed. My gaze moves over the shadows in the room until I find him against the wall, his shadow thumbing through my textbook. "Don't touch that."

He flips the book open to a page, pale white from the moonlight through the blinds. "To prove an identity, you have to use logical steps to show that one side of the equation can be transformed into the other side of the equation. You know what that means, Penny?"

I'm supposed to feel bad for stealing his money, and I do, but right now I'm mad. Mad that he wasn't there and mad that he suddenly appeared. Mad that he scared me.

"Yeah, I know what it means. Probably more than you."

His laugh sounds so much like the man from school that I narrow my eyes, looking at the way he holds his head, the way his shoulders are set, the way he carries himself. Same, same, same. "You some kind of baby genius?"

"I'm not a baby."

"And I'm the dumbass who left you with my

money."

My cheeks turn hot. "I'm sorry I did that. I have it here, under my pillow. The rest of it, anyway. After I paid for the soup. But you can have that too, if you want."

He laughs, the sound clanging like bells. "I don't want it back."

"You have to take it," I say, scared that he sounds so much like that stranger. "The soup is enough for me, if you leave it. And you need the money more than I do."

His shadow goes still. "What do you know about that?"

"I know you have a dad who's mean, mean enough to run away from."

"Doesn't take a baby genius to figure that out. I pretty much told you."

"Then there's the man from the school."

"What school?"

"From some fancy private school, I guess. He came to visit me at recess." Something cold touches my bones, making me shiver. There's a reason his laugh sounds the same. A reason he's run away from home. The answer comes to me the way numbers do, before I'm even sure I want to know.

Black eyes narrow. "What did he look like?"

"Like you."

This strange feeling comes over me, like it did when I first cheated. I knew I had something important I needed to do. But I didn't have a deck of cards in front of me. No trigonometry proof to solve. Numbers were easy, but people are hard. They always have been.

A boy without any place to go.

A man who promises me safety, a real future.

The proof doesn't write itself inside my mind. There are gaps between each logical jump. Unsolved variables. Unknowns. I can figure out the answer anyway. It makes too much sense.

"He talk to your class?" The boy's voice is casual, but I can hear the tension underneath.

"Not really. He came at recess. I think Mrs. Keller told him what I can do."

"And what's that?"

I shrug in the dark. "Does it matter?"

"Yeah, it matters. It matters if you told him what he wanted to hear."

That dark wave passes over me again, dragging me under. A warning. "He gave me a bad feeling. Not the same as Mr. Romero, but worse. So I told him a wrong answer."

"Good. When he comes back you tell him as many wrong answers as you need to until he goes away."

"How do you know he'll come back?"

"Because he doesn't give up." A short laugh. "I thought that meant he would keep looking for me. Instead he went looking for a replacement."

"Did you go to his school?"

The sound he makes is hard and mean. "His school? Yeah, I guess you could say that. Learned a lot. You wouldn't like it there, trust me."

"They don't have the free lunch program?"

A longer pause this time. "It's important that you don't go along with him, understand? No matter what he says. No matter what he promises you. It's not worth it, okay? You need to believe me."

"I don't even know you."

He tosses the book aside. "I'm serious. You need to stay away from him."

"Tell me your name. And don't say it's Quarter."

"Why does that matter?"

"Because you want me to trust you. At least I should know what to call you."

"Damon Scott."

My stomach sinks. "So that means your dad is…"

"Jonathan Scott, yes. You've heard of him,

then. That's good. You know what he's capable of."

Everyone in the trailer park knows about him, after Lisa Blake. The people my father plays cards with are dangerous, the ones he borrows money from even more so. But even he would never dare go near Jonathan Scott, the man who rules the west side of Tanglewood.

"Why would he want me?"

"Because he likes to fuck—sorry. He likes to mess with people. That's what he does. Moves people around on his big ugly chessboard. You know how to play chess?"

I shake my head even though he can't see me. Some of the books I've read have descriptions of chess. I know how the pieces move but I've never played. Never even seen a chess set in person. "Not really."

"Well, pawns are the front line. They're easy to find, but they can only move one way, one square at a time. A kid who's what? Six years old?"

"Seven," I say, indignant.

A soft laugh. "A seven-year-old doing trigonometry. Imagine what he could turn you into."

"What?" I asked, a little awed by the idea that I could become something. Something other than one of the tired mothers with three kids from different men or one of the women on the street corners. A girl from the west side didn't have other options.

"He'd turn you into a weapon," Damon says, his voice flat. "A bullet. He would spend years making you, and when you were done, he'd pull the trigger."

"Is that what he did to you?"

"Why?" he asks, his voice rough. "Do I seem dangerous?"

I remember the way he had looked that first night, all puffed up and strong. Like he could shoot me with the gun he claimed to have. Or slash me with his knife. Instead he had offered me food.

And he didn't hurt me now, even though I'd stolen from him.

"You're not dangerous."

After a beat he says, "Not to you, baby genius. Not to you."

CHAPTER FOUR

FOR THE NEXT four days Damon lives in the trailer with me.

Mostly he disappears during the day. He isn't there when I get off the bus. But he always comes back at night. He works through the trigonometry book with me, teasing me when I get the answer right, encouraging me when I don't.

"Won't your dad lose his shit if he sees me in his bed?" he asks.

"I lock the deadbolt," I say. "Even Daddy would have to knock to get in. And I'd wake you up before I opened the door. How did you get in, anyway?"

"The kitchen window."

There's barely a foot and a half in that space. Only enough for the feral cats in the neighborhood to sneak in and have a drink from the leaky faucet and dash out again.

He doesn't act like Daddy. There are no rules and no drinking. But he does take care of me. Like a big brother, I decide. That's what it's like.

A big brother who brings food and does math with me. I can almost forget that Daddy's still missing.

I can almost forget that he might not come back.

It's on the fifth day that everything goes wrong.

Mrs. Keller calls me to her desk. "Why did you tell Mr. Scott the wrong answer?"

I shrug. *Maybe I didn't know the right answer.* She'd know that I'm lying. I can do a lot more than multiply numbers together.

Her eyebrows press together. "He has resources that we can only dream of at the school. Advanced teachers and materials." She pauses, taking a deep breath. "There would be boarding. You would have to live somewhere else. Do you understand?"

This is my way out. An escape from West Tanglewood Elementary. A chance to be someone other than the teenage mother or the girl on the street corner.

"What about you?" I ask.

Her brown eyes widen. "What about me?"

"I could do what you did. I could be a teacher."

Her nose scrunches like it does when someone

gets a wrong answer. "Penny, I don't think you realize how special you are. It's not just that you're the smartest girl at this school. You're the smartest person I've ever met, anywhere. And I wish—"

My head tilts. "You wish what?"

"I wish that you would give Mr. Scott the right answer. I convinced him to give you another chance. He's coming back tomorrow."

Curiosity sparks inside me, but it's not because of his special school. What did he do to Damon to make him run away? If he has so much money, why does Damon sleep outside?

The questions follow me home on the bus. They nip at my heels like the wild dogs that sometimes follow me around the trailer park. They keep my eyes open when I'm in bed, waiting for the soft shift of the walls that means he's come back.

I find him in the kitchen, pouring a can of soup into a bowl.

"What are you doing up?" he says without turning around.

"Couldn't sleep. Where did you go today?"

He gives me a warning look. "Around."

I sit down at the kitchen table, swinging my legs. "Fine, don't tell me. I have a secret, too."

"Do you?" The way he asks I know he thinks it's something dumb, like maybe I'm going to tell him what Jenny Carson said during gym class again. That was only one time.

"It's about you," I tell him, triumphant.

He drops the spoon into the bowl, his eyes narrowing. "What?"

My heart squeezes a little, because when he stares at me like that he reminds me too much of Jonathan Scott. "You tell me your secret first."

"This is not a fucking game. Did someone come around asking about me?"

I'm not going to budge, even though he used the f-word. "You go first."

"Jesus," he says, running his hand through his hair. He pulls some money from his pocket, tosses it on the kitchen table. "I was getting this. You don't want to know how, because it wasn't exactly legal. And I don't like going into the city because it means there's a chance I'll be seen, but this way you won't have to go wandering if your daddy doesn't come back. You'll have enough to eat, at least."

I frown, looking at the money. There's more than two hundred dollars. How could he make that much in one day? "Was it dangerous?"

He laughs, the sound sharp and short. "Tell

me your secret."

Now that it's time, I don't want to tell Damon. I'm afraid of what he'll say, what he'll think, but I can't back out now. If there's one thing I learned from going with Daddy to those poker games, it's the importance of following through on your promises.

The importance of paying your debts.

"Your daddy's coming back to the school tomorrow."

He's silent a moment, but it's not a quiet silence. It's louder and louder in the still night air, so much that when he finally speaks it sounds soft. "Say that again."

"My teacher, Mrs. Keller. She said he'll give me another chance. That I should tell him the right answers because he can help me."

"He can't help you."

"But she said—"

"I don't give a flying fuck what she told you."

"Why would she lie?"

"Because she's working for him? Because he's blackmailing her? Or maybe she thinks that no matter how bad he is it will still be better for you, but I'm telling you she's wrong."

I shrug, uncomfortable with his intensity. "I guess."

"Don't talk to him, Penny."

"He's going to talk to me at recess. What am I supposed to do?"

"Ignore him. Scream. Kick him in the balls."

"Why is he so bad?" I demand. "Why did you leave?"

"You're too little to talk about that."

"I'm not too little!"

"You are, baby genius."

"I'm not a baby," I say, making my voice as loud and strong as I can. "And anyway, you don't have to tell me. I'll just ask Mr. Scott when I see him tomorrow."

His eyes darken. "You wouldn't."

I probably wouldn't, because it would put Damon in danger—wouldn't it? Then Mr. Scott would know where to look for him. It's such a coincidence that I would even meet them so close together. The father and the son. In two totally different places. The odds had to be huge. I've calculated hundreds of odds with just fifty-two cards, but the number of people in Tanglewood is a lot more than that. Even if you narrow that down to the west side, you're still in the tens of thousands.

And with a horrible click the calculation fell into place.

I scramble up from the chair, backing away. "Why are you here?" I whisper.

"What?" Damon looks confused, but I already know he's a good liar.

"Is it some kind of trick? You tell me not to go so that I will?"

"I have no idea what you're talking about."

"Or maybe you're here in case I say no. Like if I don't go with Mr. Scott at school tomorrow you'll be here waiting for me when I get back."

"And do what?"

"I don't know! Whatever people like you do. All I know is that it's not a coincidence that I meet you and your father in the same week. It can't be."

Guilt flashes across his face. "Look, Penny."

"Don't say my name."

"It's not what you think."

"You lied to me."

"I left some stuff out."

"That's lying!"

"Okay, I lied. But not because I'm working with my dad. I swear to you." He stands and paces in the small kitchen, his expression severe. "And I'm serious about what I said. Stay away from him."

My lower lip trembles, and I bite down hard.

47

It's an old trick from when one of Daddy's poker friends starts saying things I don't like. I refused to cry in front of them.

Damon's dark eyes flash. "I knew who you were because my dad keeps tabs on everyone. On people who owe him money. On people who might be useful to him. People like you."

It's warm outside and downright hot in the trailer. The poor air conditioning unit struggles against the coming summer, certain to lose that battle. But right now, standing in my bare feet on the kitchen linoleum, I feel freezing cold. I wrap my arms around myself.

My voice is small. "That's why Daddy's been gone so long, isn't it?"

"He owed a lot of money."

"You saw him?" A knot swells in my throat. "Is he alive?"

Damon shoves his hands across his chest, looking somehow older and younger at the same time. "He was desperate, okay? You have to understand that."

I blink. "Okay."

"People like that, they see their life flashing in front of their eyes. It breaks something inside them. And my father—he loves that moment. He lives for it."

"What did he do?" I whisper.

"He starts talking about his daughter, how smart she is, all the things she can do. How you help him count cards. At first my father doesn't care. He says, *not that well since you ended up here.* But your dad explains how you aren't allowed at the high stakes games. That's where he lost all his money."

My insides feel wobbly, like I'm going to cry no matter how hard my nails press into my palm. "I don't understand. If you were there, if you saw that, why did you come here?"

He shrugs, shaking his head like he doesn't know the answer. "I meant to leave the city for good. That's what I was doing. Running. Escaping. And I almost did it. I got on a grey bus heading west and pulled my cap low. Then I found myself getting off at the first stop. Hitching a ride back. And camping behind the trailer park."

"Damon," I say, pressing my hands together. This is how you pray. "What did Mr. Scott do to you?"

"What's important is that he's never gonna do it to you, understand? I'm going to stop him."

I shake my head *no*, because I don't understand. I know Damon is strong and smart, but how is he going to stop his father? And if he had any power over him, why did he leave in the first place?

"Yes," Damon says, "but you need to keep your head down. No more reading about trigonometry. No more counting cards. That's the deal we're gonna make."

"I don't want any deal." *I don't want you to leave.*

"That's the only way you see your daddy again. If I go back."

My breath catches. "But why?"

"Because he owes a debt. You didn't replace him, but someone has to."

And then I can't stop the tears. They're hot and thick on my cheeks. I hate crying in front of him, but he doesn't look like he feels sorry for me. He has this serious expression, like he's waiting. Waiting for me to take the deal.

How can I say yes when that means sending Damon back to his father?

How can I say no when it means never seeing mine?

There's two hundred dollars on the kitchen table, but it won't last forever. Not long enough for me to be a young mother or a girl on the street corner. I'd starve before that. Or I would end up with Mr. Scott.

I shake my head, because I don't want it to be true. "You can help me find him."

"And then what? We all go on the run, one big happy family?"

His tone says that's ridiculous. He's mocking me, but it *is* what I want. "Maybe. Why is that wrong? We could be happy like that."

Those black eyes soften. "It's not possible, Penny. There's nowhere we could run, not enough money or power in the world to hide us."

"What will you do?" I whisper.

In that question is my acceptance, my apology. It would always have come to this.

He knew that before I did.

"The same thing I did before," he says with a hard smile. "Survive."

CHAPTER FIVE

THE NEXT DAY I spend most of recess in the jungle gym, in that dark, quiet place beneath the slide and behind the rusted metal wall with numbers cut out. I peer through the number eight at the door, waiting for someone to appear. No one ever does.

Mrs. Keller stares at the door, her small face hopeful. Then worried.

By the time she calls the class back inside she looks disappointed.

I don't want her to feel bad so I tug on her hand as I pass by. She bends low, and I whisper in her ear. "I don't want a new school anyway. I like you being my teacher."

She blinks like she has something in her eye.

The rest of the day I sit quiet, wondering how I'm going to play dumb. We're learning fractions right now. How do you pretend not to know something? I wish I just *didn't* know.

I wish I were normal.

When it comes time for the quiz, I take a deep

breath. This is how it has to be. It's the promise I made. So even though I know that Joey only eats 1/8th of the pizza, I write down 1/16.

There are two questions I get wrong, which means my grade will be a B. Very average.

My whole life will be average.

When I get off the bus, from across the road, I see something dark and large slumped in front of my door. Is it Damon? Is he hurt? I run as fast as I can, kicking dirt into the air, clouding my sight.

Even before I get there I know it's not him. The figure is too large.

"Daddy," I shout over the pounding of my feet.

He doesn't move. When I get close I see why. His face is swollen and bruised, dried blood caked over the right side. The sound of his breathing fills the humid air, thick with blood and snot.

"Daddy," I say again, but this time it comes out as a sob. I can't press my nails into my palm this time. Nothing will keep me from crying now.

A low sound fills the air, almost separate from the still body in front of me. Only when I put my hand to his chest and feel the faint rise and fall, the slight rumble, am I sure the sound is coming from him.

"Penny," he says, the word slurred and broken.

"I'm here," I say, fighting to keep my voice steady. One of us has to be strong.

"No, Penny. What did he—" Daddy breaks off in a fit of coughing, the sound horrible and echoing. "I'm so sorry. What did he do to you?"

He thinks Mr. Scott did something to me. That it's the reason he's free.

"Let's go inside," I say, pulling his hand.

With a groan of pain and effort, he staggers up. Only to collapse again. I catch him with both hands, my shoulders, even my neck. A shock of weight. My bones hurt, my muscles shake. I need to get him inside. We move together in a terrible dance, falling into potholes and stumbling on the stairs. The screen door slams into my hand. His head knocks against the doorframe.

When we reach the couch it's all I can do to tip him over. He falls onto the sagging cushions with a swear word. I run to the kitchen. Underneath the sink there's a first aid kit in my old lunchbox, the one with My Little Pony on the front. I pull out cotton balls and rubbing alcohol. He probably needs a hospital. What if something is broken? But this is all we have.

I pause to look at the kitchen table. The two hundred dollars isn't there anymore, tucked away under my bed instead. But I can still remember the way Damon looked sitting there, eating the soup I bought with his money. Is he okay? Is he beaten like Daddy is right now?

My eyes press shut, sending up a prayer that someone is there to take care of him.

Then I kneel at the couch.

Daddy looks more alert than he did before, his eyes less glassy and more focused. "I told him about you. About counting cards. He said he was going to—" His voice breaks.

I could tell him that Mr. Scott didn't touch me, but that won't help.

He could have. He would have, if it weren't for Damon.

"Rest now," I say in a quiet voice.

I learned my quiet voice from Mama. It's the one I used when she had been up too late, when men had been over, when she had a headache. When I brought her a glass of water and Tylenol.

She would call Daddy bad names for leaving her in this shithole trailer park. And then one day she put a needle in her arm and went to sleep. I had to spend three months in a group home, keeping my head down and hiding the bruises from the other kids.

Then they found Daddy. I know he isn't

perfect but he's the only person I have left. Tears trail down my cheeks, but I don't know if I'm crying for myself or for Damon, who traded himself for me.

"You saw him, Penny?"

I look down. "He's tall. And his voice—it's strange. Like water."

Daddy's face falls. "Oh God. I'm so sorry."

Maybe it's mean to let him think the worst, but I need him to change. The debts and the gambling, those are his needles. And I don't want him to go to sleep, not like Mama did.

I don't want to sleep either.

And I stay awake long after Daddy snores, the pain medicine keeping him comfortable. The shadows of trees press against my window. Somewhere out there is a lake. Somewhere out there is a boy who knows how to hold his breath longer than anyone should. How did he learn that?

What is he learning now?

I'm so sorry, Daddy said. But I'm the one who's sorry.

Because Damon Scott traded himself for me. He's the only reason I'm safe.

And I'm the reason he's not.

CHAPTER SIX

I T GETS EASIER to pretend as time goes by. My mind applies itself to finding an appropriate percentage to get wrong as easily as it did counting cards.

Daddy kept down a job long enough that we could move into the west side from the trailer park. The apartment was smaller than the trailer, but this way I could visit my friends after school. As it turns out, people like you when you keep your mouth shut and get average grades.

I was almost popular, but no one knew who I really was.

Damon Scott's name became a part of the city's dark culture, mostly in whispers, always linked to money or women or both. No one really seemed surprised that he had gone into the family business, that he traded in sex and violence. Even I wasn't surprised, knowing what had happened, but I did mourn him. He could have run away, if it hadn't been for me.

Then again, he's a grown man now, wealthy

in his own right.

He could run away now, if he wanted to.

There must be something he likes about that life, something dark and sharp he's addicted to. We all have our own needles. We each rack up our own debts.

Sometimes Daddy would slip. Bills would pile up, only for him to dig us out again. When we got close to getting evicted I would count cards, but only once. Then twice. He was as scared of Jonathan Scott as me, so he understood the risk.

And I had my own addiction. Stolen moments in the Mathematics section of the high school library. Fractals drawn on my school notebooks, filled in with little hearts and smiley faces so that no one would suspect anything. No one ever did.

Once Mr. Halstead asked me to stay after physics, where he told me that I wasn't living up to my potential. He seemed so sincere, so kind, that I actually agreed to come to after school study sessions with him. But when he put his hand on my leg and breathed against my neck, I knew he didn't really care about my mind.

It wasn't anything special about me that they liked.

Only that I was a girl in the west side. We

were only used for one thing.

And then there was Brennan. He had a crooked smile and a motorcycle, so all my friends thought he was a great catch. I could see the appeal, from an academic standpoint. His muscles were sharpened from working in his father's garage, his confidence an attractive quality. I hoped he never found out I went out with him for his books. *Automotive Wiring and Electrical Systems. Advanced Automotive Fault Diagnoses.* Not my ideal form for numbers to take, but I read them with the same secret fervor that my father bought lotto tickets, both of us desperate for a fix.

"What are you reading, babe?"

I slammed shut his book on hybrid vehicles and slipped it under my open book from Calculus class. Technically math, but it had less to teach me than *See Spot Run.* Brennan's a nice guy.

Nice enough I hope he never finds out I'm using him for his books.

"Studying," I tell him, rising up to kiss him.

He's sweaty from working. Their house is next door to the garage. "You hungry? I'll shower and then we can go somewhere."

"I have a shift at eight." I work at a sad little diner, making five bucks an hour serving barely heated food and stale coffee. It's better than most jobs a fifteen-year-old girl can get in west Tanglewood.

"Thought you had Fridays off."

"Jessica's baby has a fever."

Brennan sighs. "We barely get to go out."

Guilt rises inside me, because I kind of prefer it that way. Hanging out after school and making out on his couch. Every time we go to a party it's another chance to take things further.

Brennan wants that. Maybe even deserves it, after being so patient. But I can't give it to him. Can't end up like Jessica with a baby. I don't think Brennan would bail the way Jessica's boyfriend did, but it's too big of a risk.

I put my hand on his arm. "I'm sorry. I couldn't say no." *And I didn't want to.* "Besides, you know I need the money."

Something flashes across his eyes. Frustration. Futility? "What will you make? Twenty bucks? I could give you that if you spent the night."

My hand snatches back. "Excuse me, I'm not for sale."

"I didn't mean it like that. I mean the job's total shit and you know it."

"Well it's the only one I have." I whirl away so he can't see the hopelessness on my face. There's only so much humiliation a girl can take in one evening. I stare out his window at the rows of dark windows, the broken bricks. The west side is a tumbled-down maze, not even fit for living, keeping us trapped.

There is no exit strategy. No way out.

Brennan's arms wrap around me, slick and dirty with grease but comforting all the same. "I'm a fucking idiot," he murmurs into my hair. "I know you're doing the best you can."

"I just want to…" *Escape. Fly to the moon.* "Graduate. Then we can make plans."

"Okay," he says, because he understands my desire to finish school. He has his GED and he's studying to get certified as an automotive technician. He's a high achiever among our friends. And he'll never know that my dreams are so far beyond this.

That I long for the impossible.

"I should get going. I have to change first."

He turns me in his arms, his strong hands warm with familiarity, painful with certainty. He presses a kiss to my mouth. I part my lips, and he takes the invitation, pressing his tongue inside, opening me. I let him, let him, let him. That's all I know how to do anymore.

I like his kisses the same way I like boxed mac and cheese and my worn mattress at home. They mean I'm safe and comfortable, if not quite happy.

He pulls back like he always does. Maybe sensing I would finally snap if he pushed.

It's his own form of safe and comfortable.

His eyes search me. What does he want to find?

He traces my eyebrow, his finger agreeably callused. His expression is a little awed. "You're the prettiest girl in the west side, you know that?"

"And out of the west side?" I ask, not because I'm vain enough to think I am. Because I want to know when we resigned ourselves to this. When we noticed the iron bars around our lives and decided not to rail against them.

His smile is sad and tired. "Out of the west side you wouldn't be with me."

It's an arrow straight to the heart, because he's right. And he deserves better. Don't we both? I throw my arms around him and squeeze. We need friends in captivity.

BRENNAN TAKES ME home on his motorcycle, the roar of the engine bouncing off pavement and brick. I mold myself to his body, my eyes squeezed tight in his helmet. There's a perverse thrill as we race through the darkened streets. Both of us know this is as fast and as far as we'll ever go. One slip on slick gravel is all it would take. And the worst part is the faint sense that we're waiting for it. Wanting it. Pushing the boundaries in the hopes that we leave on our own terms, young and free.

We arrive at my apartment building, sudden stillness almost violent after the rush.

The crumbling concrete of the curb shifts under my feet.

My ears ring as I take off the helmet, placing it on Brennan's head and tapping it into place. "I dub thee Sir Brennan. Go forth into battle."

He grins from beneath the visor. "If I'm a knight, what does that make you?"

"The princess, of course."

Kissing never works well with a helmet on. Someone's forehead ends up smacked. Instead I kiss my palm and press it to his mouth, the way lords and ladies did with handkerchiefs.

A chaste kiss.

Then he's off in a cloud of exhaust, his noble steed lovingly restored and shining.

The diner is only a couple blocks away. I have plenty of time to change before my shift. Then it will be a monotony of grease and coffee, miles to go on the same black-and-white tiles with my tired feet.

I turn toward my building, mentally bracing myself for the night to come.

"Hello, princess."

The words come out of the dark alley to the side, and I jump back. Brennan insists on taking me home every night, when I could take the bus, partly because of safety. The voice is low and grave and completely new to me. If it's a stranger the best thing I can do is ignore him. Hope he goes away.

That's what they tell you to do about bullies, isn't it?

I put my head down, wrapping my arms around myself.

With my eyes downcast I can't see him, but I feel him. He steps out of the shadows, his presence like a cold burst of air in the hot night. "That's not what I call you, though. To me you'll always be a baby genius."

Shock holds me paralyzed on the sidewalk. A dangerous prospect considering it's late in the evening in the west side. Made even more dangerous because I know exactly who this is.

I know exactly what he's become.

There's a storm inside me. A whirlwind of

surprise and fear, threatening to drown me. *Why are you back?* That's what I want to ask. From somewhere deep inside, another whisper. *Why did you take so long?*

"It's so much more interesting than a princess, don't you think? A pretty face has its appeal, but a sharp mind is a goddamn aphrodisiac."

When I turn to face him, he moves behind me. "I don't know what you're talking about."

He makes a *tsk* sound, keeping pace as I try to confront him. "That's not true, Penny. But I understand. You're so used to playing dumb, aren't you? It's more than a habit now. It's a veil, keeping you hidden."

"I can't believe you're talking to me right now."

"You don't have to hide with me."

"I'm not trying to hide," I say, and with him at least it's the truth. "I'm trying to look at you."

He stops moving, and I finally face him.

I must have turned one too many times, because the air leaves my chest. Nothing could have prepared me for the sight of his dark eyes—black like night. Like inky depths I could never hope to enter. Never hope to escape. He looks so much like his father it steals my breath.

Some logical part of me knows they have

differences. Jonathan Scott already had silver threading his dark hair when I met him years ago. He was taller, leaner, more severe in every way. It's my heart that's somehow breaking, seeing in him the whisper of evil.

With his perfectly disarranged hair and the evening shadow on his jaw, he bears little resemblance to the wild boy I knew once. His lips have filled out. His chest has filled out too, fitting into that dress shirt and tailored vest perfectly. Only the eyes prove it's him, at once knowing and curious. Pitch black, like the night sky above the city, no stars at all to light the way.

I think I loved him once.

About as much as I despise this handsome man. He's everything my mother would have chased after. Everything I've learned not to trust.

"You're right," he says softly. "We should go up."

"You're not going anywhere with me." I glare at him, giving him my meanest look. It doesn't seem to worry him any. A smile flickers on his lips, making him look dashing.

I don't trust men who look dashing.

Amusement flashes across dark eyes, as if he knows. "Where are your manners?"

"They're reserved for people I actually like."

"Like Brennan Chase?"

I struggle to remember if I said Brennan's full name. *I dub thee Sir Brennan. Go forth into battle.* My heart squeezes, imagining Damon keeping tabs on me. "How do you know his last name?"

"It's my business to know people's names. Their likes and dislikes. Their addictions. Do you have any addictions, baby genius?"

"Do you?"

"Many. Some worse than others."

An answer that admits nothing. "What are you doing here?"

"I may not deserve a warm welcome, but I didn't expect hostility. You invited me inside once."

"That was before you were your father's puppet." I still feel guilty for that, but it doesn't change the fact that he can't be trusted. He didn't only survive his father. He became him.

"Ah."

"That's all you have to say for yourself?"

"Would you like me to deny it? Fine. That's not true, darling. I was most definitely my father's puppet before we ever met."

The seductive tone almost draws me in, even as his words confirm my worst fears. "You did what you had to do when you were a child. You're a grown man now."

"Thank you for noticing. Though I don't work with my father."

"Everyone says you do."

"They say that?"

"They say you deal in money and drugs and women."

He pauses meaningfully. "Not with my father, I don't."

It's an admission.

He does every horrible thing he's accused of doing. Every single thing I raged against in my mind. How could the sweet boy I once met be so horrible? How could someone who once risked his life for me be responsible for hurting other girls?

All the street lamps have blown out here, maybe on purpose. The only light is the moon, and when it shines over his dark eyes, the reflection makes them look silver.

He may not work with his father, but he's become him.

"And that's supposed to make it better?" I manage to ask. "That you do them for your own gain instead of working for your father?"

"Better? No, but it's definitely more lucrative this way."

It's upsetting that he looks so clean and crisp and *beautiful* standing beside a run-down tenement. Upsetting that he looks so good when he's clearly a bad man. That his movie star smile hides a terrible broken soul. "You're not the boy I knew."

"No," he agrees. "Are you the girl I knew?"

"You'll never find out."

He tilts his head to the side, as if demurring. Too much of a gentleman to tell me I'm wrong. Except he's no gentleman. "What are you doing here?"

"I came to speak to your father."

My heart thuds. "Why?"

"He owes me money."

Oh God. *Daddy, what have you done?* "He doesn't."

I'm only delaying the inevitable, but I can't think right now. Can't deal with the fact that we have rent due in two days and barely enough money to cover it. How will we pay back hundreds of dollars?

Damon looks to the side a little. As if he's embarrassed by my horror. Or maybe bored. He straightens the cuffs of his fine white shirt, perfectly tailored to his broad chest and narrow waist. He might be waiting in the eaves for an opera to begin, so casually refined.

"How dare you?" I whisper, waiting for him to meet my eyes, daring him.

He glances back at me, one dark eyebrow raised. "Pardon?"

"You know he doesn't have a way to pay you back. How dare you loan him money? Charging insane interest rates he'll never be able to afford. How dare you?"

A small laugh. "Would you have preferred I told him no? He would have gone straight to my father, who would have charged him higher interest than I did."

"I hate you," I say, tears stinging my eyes. "I hate you both."

"And it's not quite true that he doesn't have a way to pay the money back."

The silence spins out in brutal possibility. "How?"

"He has you."

PART TWO

THE KING

CHAPTER SEVEN

WHEN I FIRST came to live with Daddy he worked in a prison-release program at Goodwill. He would pick things out of the donation piles to bring home. A Barbie with her hair cut jagged. A half-empty box of tinker toys. It was when he brought home the Rubik's Cube that we hit the jackpot.

Some of the stickers had been torn or smudged away, but the colors were still visible. Only one sticker was gone completely, but a quick count of the sides told me it was yellow.

I sat down in front of the armchair, still worn and lumpy then. My legs crisscrossed, my heart pumping. And in twenty minutes solved the cube for the first time.

Daddy watched with a strange look in his eyes.

When I was done he turned the columns this way and that, trying his best to make sure no two colors were side by side. This time I already had practice. It took fifteen minutes.

So many evenings we sat like that, him messing up the cube, me putting it right.

That was before he lost the job at Goodwill, before he turned heavy to gambling. Before I met Damon Scott and began to hide what I could do.

Though I guess we're still in old patterns. Daddy messing things up.

Me putting it right.

I can tell Daddy's home before I put my key in the lock. Something about the air feels heavy with despair, with guilt—though maybe that's just wishful thinking. I want him to be sorry for what he's done. But the only thing I feel when I feed my addiction, when I breathe in the sharp tang of numbers is relief.

He sits in his lumpy armchair, the secondhand metal cane leaning against the side.

My feet seem to slow down as I approach him. As much as I need to have this confrontation, as many questions and accusations are swirling inside me, I wish I were anywhere but here.

I don't bother to sit on the lumpy couch or the wooden coffee table with a crack down the side. Instead I sit down at his feet, crossing my legs. In the same place I sat so many times. The same way I did when I was a little girl.

That's how I feel right now. Small and help-less.

In Daddy's eyes I find terrible confirmation.

"I'm sorry," he says gruffly.

"I don't understand. Why would you borrow from Damon Scott?" When his lips press together, my heart stops. "Oh God. You owe someone else."

He shakes his head, as if struggling to under-stand it himself. "I thought if I could pay off the debt with Damon Scott I'd have more time. So I borrowed from someone else. Pretty soon I owed almost everyone in the city money."

"Almost?" I say, my voice tight.

Where I felt a surge of emotion with Damon Scott, there's only emptiness. A blissful numbness that spreads from my heart to my fingers. It's a relief, however temporary.

His eyes sharpen. "I didn't borrow from Jona-than Scott."

"You wanted to."

"It doesn't matter anyway, whether I bor-rowed from him or not. There's no way I can survive this. Not with the amount of money on the line."

"Damon Scott talked to me."

Daddy surges up in a surprising show of

strength, before making a cry of pain and falling back into the chair. "That bastard. Did he touch you?"

That small amount of protectiveness makes my heart squeeze. This is what I wanted. Someone to care about me, someone for me to care about. Without having to worry about kneecaps breaking.

How is it that some people get huge trees of family, aunts and uncles and cousins? A flick of a DNA strand, a twist of fate. And here I am, almost alone. Except for one person.

I can't quite meet that person's eyes. "Damon might be willing to help."

"He's no better than his father," Daddy snarls. "Leaning on family like that. He's not supposed to do that. He's never done it before. And with you still a child."

A child? Not really. There are enough men in the diner who stare at me to know they see me as a woman. And Jessica's barely older than me, her body just as slender despite having given birth only eight months ago. We grow up early in the west side.

The Rubik's Cube is long gone, lost to the vagaries of childhood. Maybe left behind in the trailer outside of town. But my fingers clench together all the same, longing for something to solve.

A puzzle that's guaranteed to have an answer.

"What will we do?" I ask softly.

"I have a plan," he says, gruff, almost glad.

"But how—"

"It's better if you don't know."

"Tell me."

"There's this big game."

Dread slithers down my spine, thick and cold. "No way."

"The pot is huge, Penny. It could pay off all the debts and still have more."

"You have to win."

"With your help I would. If you were there—"

"You don't think anyone would notice?" Counting cards isn't allowed, which has never made sense to me. As if I could *stop* counting them. But any sort of signals I made would definitely be caught.

"The game isn't for six months," he says. "We have plenty of time to practice them."

"And what would I be doing at a high-stakes game?" Even in the twisted sex world of Tanglewood, the fifteen-year-old daughter of a player would not be allowed into the private room. There are rules, which is why I couldn't help him in the big games.

He's silent in that way that's filled with words. With guilty admissions. "You'd be in the room if you were my buy-in."

My gasp sounds loud and ridiculously innocent in the broken little apartment. Who knew I still had naivete to shatter? "You want to bet me?"

"It costs fifty thousand dollars just to enter."

Oh my God. I thought we had hit the bottom with the debts, but this is worse. There are rocks down there, sharp and slick. And no one to pull me from the water.

Suddenly I remember Damon Scott, his eyes black, fierce.

What made him able to hold his breath underwater so long?

My throat tightens. The memory of a tall man in black sweeps over me, his grey eyes like mist in a dream. "Who's running the game, Daddy?"

"Jonathan Scott."

"Don't do this," I whisper, knowing I'm too late.

"We'll win, Penny." He's pleading now, asking forgiveness for something already decided. We're not so far away from medieval times. A man can sell his daughter. A man can gamble her.

I don't have to ask what happens if he loses,

my body forfeit.

Horror is a black hole, threatening to drag me under. Only denial keeps me floating in endless space, denial that my own daddy would do this. "There has to be another way."

He stares at his hands, knotted together. I know he has arthritis, that his joints swell up in the warm muggy nights, that he struggles to hold the cards.

Oh God, I hate that I care about him.

"The debts are coming due," he says, and in his voice I hear the grains of sand falling, the amount of time I'm the owner of my body slipping away. The water level rising.

CHAPTER EIGHT

THE DINER STILL pays me off the books, the way they did before I was old enough to legally work. That means I get to keep one hundred percent of my measly tips, the handful of coins tired factory workers leave beside their empty coffee cups.

Supposedly I'm saving for college, but both Daddy and I know that the few hundred dollars in my account will never cover actual tuition. Stochastic calculus is just a pipe dream, stored on a shelf alongside *leaving west Tanglewood* and *finding out I'm secretly a lost princess.*

Six hundred dollars seems to be the tipping point. That's how much I can save before Daddy gambles again and needs help paying the debt. A fifty-dollar note from the bar owner. A few hundred dollars deep. Not thousands of dollars.

I guess I should be flattered that I'm worth that much.

There's a cold, hard stone where that flattery would be. Polished smooth from years of being objectified and diminished, shined with every day working in this diner.

I wipe the cracked countertops with extra fervor.

"What do you recommend?" comes a voice out of my nightmares.

A muffled shriek escapes me before I catch myself.

Damon Scott sits on one of the stools, looking at ease despite the fact that his suit costs as much as a car. He sounds so much like his father that I'm surprised to see him there. And relieved. *And secretly so very glad.*

A lock of dark hair falls onto his forehead, effortlessly perfect. He studies me with a bland expression, the only sign of life the amusement dancing in his ebony eyes.

I glare at him. "What are you doing here?"

"I haven't eaten dinner."

"So go somewhere else. Somewhere with caviar and steak on gold plates."

He sighs, woebegone. "Those places can't fill a man up."

"Get out."

"I'm a great tipper."

"How about you tip the amount my father owes you?"

"I don't know." He sounds thoughtful. "That's a lot of money. And so far you haven't really given me great service."

"I'm not *servicing* you at all. Leave."

"We didn't finish our conversation."

"That's because I don't want to talk. Or see you, ever again."

"How disappointing for you."

His smug dismissal sends a jolt of electricity through my body, not entirely unpleasant. I whirl away from him and push into the kitchen. I hate how aware I am of Damon's voice, the low and sensual timbre. I hate how I can see his cocky smile even when he's not there.

The scowl on my face must be fierce because the stoic cook, Jackson, raises an eyebrow.

"What?" I demand.

He doesn't answer, just flips a greasy burger on a grill caked with black.

Ruth Mae has no such qualms. She heads out of the office like a bull seeing red, as if she can sense an unsatisfied customer from far away. If anyone on the floor gave her attitude she would throw him out in a heartbeat. That's why she doesn't usually talk to customers. Bad for business.

"What the hell are you doing?" she growls.

"Checking on an order." That's a lie but luckily Jackson slides the burger onto a bun, and I grab the plate. It takes some time to do the rounds to all my tables, to refill coffee and jot down orders.

And then there's nothing left to do but face him.

I slump behind the counter, closing my eyes. "Why are you still here?"

"Still in conversation," he says, taking a sip from his mug.

"Where did you even get that? I didn't give you coffee."

"I went behind the counter. You seem busy."

I'm replacing Jessica, but Delaney called in sick. That probably means she's high with her lame boyfriend-of-the-week. So I'm working the tables by myself. Busy is an understatement. "You have thirty seconds to finish the conversation."

One eyebrow rises up. If anything his voice becomes lower, a faint Southern drawl inflecting his dark velvet voice. "You were polite to the asshole who wanted five refills."

"They're unlimited."

"He only drank that much coffee so he could stare at your rack."

That's probably true. "Well, then he'll suffer

plenty when he finds out what five cups of that radioactive sludge does to your stomach lining."

Damon pushes the mug with his fingertip. "Duly noted."

"Is that why you're here? To stare at my rack?"

He manages to look affronted, which is a major feat for a man in his position. For a man who's put me in this position. "You're fifteen."

"Then why did you really come here?"

For once in his life he actually seems uncertain. Almost nervous. Except he has the upper hand in every possible way. He's handsome. Smart. Rich. And for some reason he's holding his breath. "Look, Penny. It isn't exactly safe for you here."

"Is that a threat? Because the last guy my dad owed money to showed up at our apartment with a baseball bat. I didn't know subtlety was part of your profession."

His eyes narrow. "His name."

"What?"

"The name of the person who showed up with a bat."

I'm not going to tell him who beat the door in, who smashed my father's knee. And I'm not going to tell him about the big poker game. This man is nothing to me. I owe him nothing. Least of all the truth.

I brace my hands on the cracked countertop, sure that I'll need the support. "How much?"

"We should talk about this in private."

Then he shouldn't have showed up at the diner. "I could shove you into the freezer?"

"He borrowed five grand. And the interest on that's... not negligible."

All the blood drains from my head. I'm dizzy with fury, impotence. Hopelessness. "Is that all?" I manage to choke out.

"No, he came back and borrowed another five."

Ten thousand dollars. My throat feels thick. I can't start crying in the middle of the diner. Ruth Mae would definitely dock my already-slim paycheck. I press my nails into my palm, counting slowly until the moment passes.

There's a look of genuine sympathy on Damon's stupidly handsome face, which makes everything worse. I want him to look smug and gloating. I want him to be easy to hate. "Penny," he says, low and grave. "I'm trying to help you."

I make a sharp motion with my hand. "If you really want to help me, stop loaning money to my dad. No matter what he wants, no matter what he promises. We'll find a way to pay you back, and then we're done."

"It's not that simple."

"Why?"

"Because your dad's fucking desperate," he says, speaking more rapidly. He runs a hand through his hair with what's most likely frustration, but it only succeeds in making him look charming. Is this what my prince looks like? No, my prince was the wild boy through the trees. "He would have gone to my father next. He would have lost everything."

"We haven't already?" I ask, bitter with grief.

"I prefer to think not," he says, his voice casual, but I'm not fooled. It matters to him what I think. It matters that I don't see him as punishment.

Tiredness sweeps over me, the weight of a thousand anxious days and a thousand sleepless nights. "I'll talk to my dad. We'll figure something out."

"It's too late for that. He'll never come up with that kind of money."

"Then what do you suggest?" I snap, my voice wavering.

"You pay the debt."

I hold up my hands, as if they can encompass

the griminess of the diner, the sadness of the west side. The complete worthlessness of my person. "With what?"

"With yourself."

His meaning comes to me like a cold, hard slap. With my body. Whether he'll use me himself or put me in one of his strip clubs, the result is the same. I'll be wrung out as surely as the girls on the street. "No," I whisper.

"You have to," he says, leaning closer.

"Or what?"

"How do you see this playing out, Penny? You work your ass off to make five hundred bucks, barely a dent in the debt. And meanwhile Daddy's out borrowing more money, from men more dangerous than myself."

"He won't," I whisper, but we both know he will.

"The city is dangerous."

"A guy slammed someone's head into the bathroom floor last Tuesday. I know it's dangerous."

His eyes turn quicksilver. "More than that. You're a target, Penny."

God. My voice comes out shaky. "Do you know what it cost me?"

A pause. "What?"

"To hide everything I'm interested in, everything I can do. Everything I am. It cost me everything. And now you want me to pay ten grand. Fine. But I'm not going to be your whore, Damon Scott. I'm keeping my dignity. That's the one thing I won't give up."

"It doesn't have to be like that."

This is a man who loves slick packaging—his European suit and his fancy watch that glints in the dim light of the diner. Except I know what's underneath, what it really boils down to, and it's not pretty. "Will I be able to come and go as I please? Will you touch me? Kiss me?"

A weighted pause. "Eventually."

"That's my dignity," I say, my voice sharp.

The corner of his mouth kicks up. "Not if I make you like it."

I meet his eyes with a solemn vow, because this is the only part of me that's left. I already gave up everything else for this dubious safety. "No," I tell him. "Never."

Frustration flits beneath his calm surface. Even a hint of vulnerability. How many people can see it? I know that not everyone sees the kind side of him. He has weapons and suits and a million kinds of armor, all designed to shield his humanity.

Assuming he has any left.

"I'll give you a little time," he says, his voice tight. "You can think it over. Weigh the lack of options. Come to terms with what you have to do. But I swear to God you'll be mine."

The words are a cold gust of wind, the tap of a branch on a window. The distant howl of a coyote at night. "No."

He looks almost compassionate as he tells me, "You don't have a choice."

He moves forward, one millimeter, as if he might touch me. Then stops.

I freeze, every part of me still and waiting. Wanting things I shouldn't. The only thing moving right now is my chest, the rise and fall so marked as we become statues.

And then his hand rises. I should duck away. Anything, anything.

My heart thuds heavy against my ribs. Two knuckles. That's the only part of his body that touches mine, at the top curve of my cheek. He strokes down in what could almost be innocent comfort.

Except that he doesn't stop at my jaw.

His knuckles slide lower, to the tender skin of my neck. To the hollow at my throat.

When his hand finally falls away, I suck in an

audible breath. He didn't touch me anywhere that would make this dirty, but my body still hums like a car left running. Nowhere to go from here.

He leaves me in that diner feeling like I've transformed.

There are crescent moons left on my palm, tinted red from breaking the skin. I wash my hands. Force myself to breathe even. I have an entire shift to get through. Every coffee cup in the diner is empty after that little chat. I have work to do, shitty tips to earn, even though they won't make a difference. Nothing I make will ever be enough.

Damon's words ring in my ear, long after he's left the diner.

A promise. A prayer. *I swear to God you'll be mine.*

CHAPTER NINE

WHEN I PLAYED dumb on the elementary school playground, I didn't fully understand what I was turning down. Mrs. Keller made it sound wonderful, a school with all the math problems I could ever dream about, a place with teachers who paid attention to me. I felt the dark undercurrent, the same way I did on that river. Every muscle in my body clenched tight, my breath coming fast.

As I got older there were other men. Other offers.

I learned to put a name on what I wanted. Freedom. The freedom to decide where I go and when. The freedom to say who can touch me. The freedom to say *no.*

Some days I wondered if it was pointless to fight the currents. This is what the dark streets did to a girl. This is how they pushed us along, eddies swirling around us, sharp rocks at the bottom.

And like that day in the tube I fought the pull.

I pumped my legs as hard as I could, even if I knew I'd go under.

I put on my uniform and go to the diner, because that's the way I swim here. My only source of money. And the whole time my mind whirs, working on other options, some loophole. Worrying at the problem until the edges are raw. My brain has done things, improbable things, almost impossible things. And now it fails me?

When the bell over the door rings at midnight I barely register the sound.

The air changes in the diner. Even the drunks and the exhausted truck drivers from out of town straighten in their seats. Ruth Mae ducks back into the kitchen. I know who it is before I turn around.

Jonathan Scott.

He's sitting in the corner booth, soft as velvet, his edges undefined. I know he's a man, flesh and blood, bone and ill-intent, but he seems somehow unreal. As if he's made of smoke.

I grab the pot of coffee and cross the diner. He won't see me cower. He won't see me beg. I give him my bland waitress smile as I pour. "What can I get you?"

He glances at the counter, where I can feel four men resolutely *not* looking at him. He exudes a menace that's unmistakable, enough to make men his size stiffen in fear.

"What kind of pie?" he asks, his voice mild.

"Peach." Ruth Mae's one concession to decent food. She makes them herself.

"I'll have that." Of course he will.

I give him a tight smile before returning to the counter. Only there do I exhale. Being around him is like being underwater. He steals all the air, all the space. Until I'm drowning.

There are other customers that want refills and plates cleared. That's my excuse for not returning right away. But really it's because I need to be away from him the same way I need oxygen.

When I cut a slice of pie, quick, sloppy, I take a deep breath.

All I want to do is slide the plate onto his table and leave.

"What's your name?" he asks.

Trapped. "Penny."

"How long have you been working here, Penny?"

The way he says my name, it sounds perverse. Like something dirty.

I don't want to tell him. I don't want to talk to him at all, but ignoring him feels like turning my back on a rabid animal—he would go in for the kill. "Two years."

That's not exactly true. I worked here longer in the back, scrubbing dishes so no one would know they had a kid working here. When I turned fifteen I got upgraded to waitress. Most people know I'm underage. No one cares.

He nods towards his coffee, still black in the mug. "I prefer two creams. Three sugars."

This isn't Starbucks. He has a mug and a little plastic tray with non-dairy creamer and sugar, like everyone else. Except we both know he isn't like everyone else.

My muscles are pulled taut, like the strings holding up a tent. About to snap. I reach for the tray, pulling out the creams, the sugars. He looks at me like it's something obscene, pulling open the creams, tearing the corners of the sugars. It feels obscene, watching the white enter the black.

He's unnaturally still, yet completely relaxed. Not quite human. Definitely not sane.

I find myself filling the silence of his body, my movement jerky and too fast in the face of this statue. I grab a spoon and stir, disturbed by the way I'm obeying silent commands. I don't mean to do that. There's something about him that compels me. An innate power. Or maybe plain old survival.

"Is that—" My throat gets tight. It's hard to stand in front of him, feeling naked. Exposed. "Is that everything?"

His eyes are a clear grey, giving the impression I can see deep inside them. "What time do you get off?"

Men ask me that question all the time. Every night. Every hour. It's just a habit, I think, for some men to proposition a girl of a certain age that they come near. Others think that a few bucks in tip means I'll meet them behind the dumpster.

Most of the time I tell them I have a boyfriend. It's the truth and it shuts them up, usually. Maybe it's shitty that I need to resort to that excuse, that a simple *no, thank you* doesn't suffice. Living in the west side you learn how to work within the system, because God knows you can't change it.

Only, I don't want to tell this man about Brennan.

That feels like a challenge he would be too glad to accept.

"That's not really—"

"Appropriate? I'm rarely appropriate."

I was going to say that it wasn't any of his business. Except that's also a challenge he would be glad to accept. There's nothing I can say, no way that I can fight him that won't make him hit harder. "I'll come back and check on you in a little bit."

"I'd rather you sit down with me."

I take a step back, moving on pure instinct. A flinch away from fire. "Please stop."

Strangely enough, he listens. He lets me run into the kitchen, where I huddle in a corner until Ruth Mae bodily shoves me back onto the floor. The corner booth is empty.

Beside the mug of coffee and the slice of pie, there's a hundred-dollar bill.

Because this isn't about money. That's what he's saying with that tip. That he has more money than God. That he doesn't need whatever pennies I can put together.

It was never really about money, was it?

It's always been about ownership.

He's the king of this godforsaken land. He can have anything he wants. Me.

CHAPTER TEN

A FTER LEAVING THE diner I visit Jessica to give her my tips for the night. It was supposed to be her shift anyway, I figure, and she and her baby need the cash more. It's not like this money is going to make a dent in the debt. She's sympathetic about the news, but not very surprised.

"You know what you should do," she says. "You should move in with Damon Scott. Like really wrap him around your little finger."

"Absolutely not."

I haven't worked so hard, fought so long, *hidden myself away* only to belong to someone else. When I was six years old I could have proved to Jonathan Scott what I could do, if I wanted to be owned by a dangerous man. Now I'm fifteen. Only three more years until I can leave Tanglewood.

"Would it really be so bad? He's hot, at least."

"I wouldn't even know how to wrap someone around my little finger."

She shrugs. "I could give you some tips."

I force myself to stay calm, to relax my hands so I don't squish the baby I'm holding. Luckily little Ky is more interested in a dragon that lights up than our conversation. "I don't know. Maybe the game is the safest bet. If I help Daddy win."

Jessica applies rouge to her perfectly contoured cheek. Her hair is flat-ironed flawlessly, her eyes sparkling. It's something she does when I come over, because I can hold Ky. And she needs to feel pretty, she says, even if she's only going to stay inside.

It's the only way she can get fifteen minutes to shower.

Her eyes meet mine in the mirror. "And if you don't win?"

My stomach drops. "Then I'm screwed. Literally."

She turns to face me, leaning back against the counter. The look on her face, the grief, like I'm already gone, it rips me to shreds. And I'm looking at her, already in pieces. She's always been like this, as long as I've known her. We're mirror images of each other. The same.

"You have to take what you can get, for as long as you can get it," she says, her voice soft and earnest. "Right now you're young. You're pretty.

That's enough to keep Damon Scott for a few weeks."

A knot forms in my throat. "That's the coldest thing I've ever heard."

"He treats his girls good."

Treats, like we were dogs. Like I'm a pet. I refused to do tricks for the father. I'm not going to start for his son. "I don't care. He still wants to own me."

She meets my gaze in the mirror. "Better than my pimp treated us, that's for sure."

My stomach drops. "Oh, Jessica. I'm so sorry."

She gets up from the stool and takes Ky, her smile sad. "Don't be sorry. You haven't done anything wrong. But I'm worried. Worried that you'll fight Damon even if he's the lesser of two evils."

The lesser of two evils. That describes him well. "Maybe you're right," I whisper.

"It's not all bad. There are always bright sides."

There's love in her blue eyes as she kisses her son's chubby cheek. His skin is darker than hers, his hair darker. He has her eyes, though, made a navy color by whatever genes his father contributed. A man I've never met. She doesn't mention him often.

"Is that what his father was?" I ask, my voice low. Low even though Ky can't understand us talking about his father. "The lesser of two evils?"

There's no judgment here. Only a dark and twisted sisterhood.

"He worked for the man my father owed money to. I was a gift. I could have said no, I guess. Could have said I wouldn't sleep in his bed, but that only would have made things harder for me."

"God, Jessica."

Her expression is deadly serious. "Don't fight them. It only makes it worse."

"I don't know if I can do that. I don't know if I can just… accept this."

"Sometimes the best way to get past something is to go through it."

This was the worst advice I could imagine, made more terrible by the fact that it was right. "What if I move in with Brennan?" I ask, grasping at straws.

"And he can protect you from these men?" she asks, the answer plain in her voice. No, he can't. And being with him would only sign his death sentence.

"There has to be another way. Anything. The

cops."

She laughs, then. "You know who dragged me back to Nico when I tried to run away? That's right. A cop."

Anger burns, old coals stoked hotter. "So much for serve and protect."

She picks up a figure with silver armor and a sword. A knight. "They serve and protect the king."

The man who owns everyone. Jonathan Scott. "Then who is Damon in this analogy?"

She shrugs. "I don't know, but I wouldn't want him for an enemy."

He's the prince, of course.

Not quite as powerful as his father, but close. Close enough to be a danger to me. They're really two sides of the same coin. Either way I'm a peasant girl in a kingdom of gilt and glamour.

Whatever Daddy did, whoever he tried to betray, the Scott family would destroy us.

"What if I don't survive?" I whisper.

"Oh honey, that's not the problem. The question you need to worry about is, what if you do?"

"MOVE IN WITH me," Brennan offers.

I blink at him from his kitchen table, the same

table where I first met his parents. "Your dad lives here."

The older Mr. Peterson is a quiet man, brooding, made even more so by the death of his wife. He works at the garage each day and late into the evening before going home to watch the nightly news. We pass nods of formality in the hallway. That's the extent of our conversation.

"He won't mind."

"He won't mind an underage girl moving in with his underage son?"

Brennan shrugs. "He knows what your dad's like. He'll understand."

Maybe he would, but I wasn't sure I could do that anymore than I could give myself to Damon Scott. Either way I would be forfeiting my life, surrendering to a man, and God, if I were used for anything at least I'd rather it was my mind.

"I don't think so. Besides, I can't leave Daddy to deal with this alone. They'll kill him."

Brennan looks unimpressed. "He's brought it on himself."

I can't help but gasp. "He's family."

"Fine." It's rare that he's ever snapped at me. He's usually easy-going, which is why we get along so well. Why we've lasted so long.

"Please," I say, putting my hand on his arm.

"I don't want you to be angry with me. I just need to figure out how to handle this. There must be something we can do. Like maybe a payment plan."

"And while time goes by, your dad's not going to gamble?"

Okay, maybe he has good reason to be mad. I'm deflated like an old balloon, its plastic stretched and small. I put my head in my hands, covering my face. "You're right. There isn't an answer."

He grimaces. "Look, I'm sorry. This is a tough situation. I know that. But the core issue isn't time, not really. It's money. You don't have anything worth that much money. And you won't, not ever."

I peek through my fingers. "Is this you trying to make me feel better?"

"Yes," he says, sounding rueful. "And not doing a good job of it. It's just—he's a heavy weight. You know? I don't want you to hold on so long he pulls you to the bottom."

The words land inside me, hard with impact. He's right, of course. Daddy's addiction will sink him. And it will sink me too, if I let it. Am I just supposed to walk away, though? I'm ashamed to admit that the thought scares me even more than it should—not only because of what would happen to Daddy. Because of what that would mean for *me*. I'd be well and truly alone in the world. And if I'm going to be underwater I'd rather hold onto an anchor than nothing at all.

"What if—" My voice cracks, though less from fear. More from a strange, dark excitement. "I know this is bad. Maybe I shouldn't even talk about it. But you're my best friend. And I have to at least consider this option—what if I paid off the debt a different way?"

It speaks to how common such ways are in the west side that Brennan doesn't ask what I mean. Sex. "That's really fucking stupid, Penny."

I flinch. Of course it is. "I shouldn't have mentioned it to you."

"You shouldn't even be considering it. There are worse things than your dad being held accountable for his debts. This could break you."

"Do I seem that fragile?"

"You're strong, Penny. But these men, they're fucking mountains. They will crush you. And they'll enjoy doing it."

He sounds so sure, as if he understands the impulse to crush me. As if he would enjoy it, too. Maybe it's inherent in men. And only the rich can indulge it. "Look, I'm not... I'm not saying I want to do it. I'm saying, isn't that option better than Daddy dying? In a totally objective way, I mean. After that we'd both be alive."

"You and your damn logic," he murmurs, but he doesn't sound angry anymore.

Only sad.

"What else is there?" I ask, honestly unsure.

"There's pride," he says.

"Yours or mine?"

He laughs a little. "I honestly don't know."

CHAPTER ELEVEN

A ND SO AFTER a week of circling the problem, a week of failed attempts to solve it, I find myself in a cab heading deep into Tanglewood. The windows are down, letting muggy air brush into the black interior. Gouges mar the plastic handles, as if someone tried to get out. And failed.

I have this sense that everything has led me to this moment.

Everything has led me to Damon Scott.

The Den is a gentleman's club, which doesn't mean there are flashing marquee lights and free buffets inside. It's an exclusive membership, where you have to know someone powerful and pay a lot of money. In other words, my father's never been inside.

I stand in front of the carved wooden door, wondering what I'll find inside. Half-naked women?

Completely naked women?

For all I know they won't even let me in the door, but I'm counting on my body to carry some weight. The same way it can be used as the entry fee to a high-stakes poker game.

The sun ducks behind the buildings, sending hot rays across my vision. It leaves the steps in shadow. I wonder if that's on purpose. A smile tugs at my lips. As if rich men can bend the elements to their will. Then again they brought me here, didn't they? As surely as rapids in the river.

The knock sounds quiet on such a heavy door. This is the historic part of downtown. There are no doorknobs. No fancy fingerprint scanner or security camera, at least not that I can see.

With a creak the door opens.

The dark silhouette is tall and familiar, the dark eyes a strange relief.

I would have expected a doorman. Maybe a bouncer. Not the man himself, his jacket missing, his shirtsleeves rolled up. He looks disheveled, as if I've pulled him out of bed.

Well, maybe I did.

"Damon Scott," I say, making my voice as hard and as haughty as I can.

He gives me a small smile. "Penny."

"I'm here to talk about my father's debt."

One dark eyebrow rises. "Do you have ten

thousand dollars? That was fast."

Of course I don't have the money. It may as well be ten million dollars, because I'll never make either amount. He doesn't even want the debt repaid, not with cash. He wants a different currency.

"Can I come inside?" I ask, hating how nervous I sound.

He could tear me down with just a sentence. With a word.

Instead he steps aside, opening the door wider. The foyer is empty. No naked women. Nothing at all except an antique side table that actually seems demure. Only in the face of such understated class do I realize fully that I expected a bordello, garish and blunt.

"Follow me," he says, turning away.

I watch his broad back, the smooth white linen. He doesn't wait for me. He doesn't have to. I hurry to keep pace with him, entering a room with plush leather chairs and a tinge of cigar smoke in the air.

"Have a seat," he says, pouring two fingers of amber whiskey into a crystal glass.

He sets it down in front of me. It makes a soft *chink* against the warm wood table.

"I'm not thirsty," I blurt out, my hands twisting together.

His handsome face is drawn into stark lines. "Tell me what you came here to say."

I had felt more sure of myself in the cab. In my bedroom, imagining Damon Scott's glinting black eyes as he told me I'd be his. Now that I'm here, my presumption seems embarrassing. My naivete even more so.

"The debt," I start, my tongue thick and ungainly. "I can pay with... Well, you know. That's what I came here to tell you. That I'll have sex with you."

"I thought you were keeping your dignity?" he asks, his voice even.

If he's surprised, he doesn't show it.

This is what I figured out while talking to Brennan. That my pride isn't about sex or money. My pride is about controlling my own fate. And that's what I'm doing here—setting the terms. This is what dignity looks like for me. Owning my own body. Deciding how it's used.

He looks down at his hands, the way they're folded together.

When he looks back up at me, his dark eyes are haunted. "I'm not my father."

There is a hot air balloon in my chest, large and rising. It feels uncomfortable to look at him, but I can't look away. "I know you aren't."

"You said I was like him, and I understand why you said that. There are things that I do, because this is the world that I operate in. But I don't hurt young women. I won't hurt you."

A strange sense of sorrow fills me. I shouldn't be sad that he's giving me time. I should throw a damn party. My heart stutters as if I'm losing something important. "Why not?"

"Does it matter? I won't press your father on the debt. You have more time now."

Unease moves through my stomach, because we're back to his terms. "How much time?"

He looks away, giving me a glimpse of his hard profile. It makes me realize how much I don't know about him. Does he have friends? Or family besides his father?

Does he have a woman upstairs?

"Long enough," he says finally.

Tension tightens the air around us, a strange pressure that builds as the seconds tick by. I should take the reprieve with a smile, but I find myself more worried than ever. "Is everything okay?"

The second the words leave my mouth I wish I could call them back. I shouldn't care about Damon Scott, even if he did protect me once.

Even if he is the most beautiful man I've ever seen.

He glances at me, his dark eyes impenetrable. "No."

One word doesn't invite more questions. My feet are rooted to the concrete, my lips forming words before I've given them permission. "Damon."

Something sharp flashes over his face. "Don't."

"Don't what?"

"Say my name."

I blink, slow and uncertain. "Why?"

"Because it's what I need to get away from. This game we're playing, the stakes are higher now. High enough that I need to leave you alone. You're not safe."

Undercurrents swirl around me, like the rapids that once pulled me under. I can sense the sharp rocks looming, the darkness closing in. "I don't understand."

"I can't want you, Penny. I can't even like you."

He wants me. "Because I'm fifteen?"

A harsh laugh. "That's not why. Do you think that could stop me? Do you think the police in this town would lift a finger to protect you from me?"

A shiver runs through me. "Stop."

He circles me on the pavement. "That's the point. This has to stop."

"You're talking in riddles," I say, turning to keep pace with him.

His voice drops lower. "That's what you like, isn't it? Riddles? Puzzles? Something that will keep that sharp mind occupied for even a second. There's been so little of that. So little mystery, hasn't there?"

I swallow hard. "You're the one who made me like this."

"I'm to blame," he murmurs, his tone sure but not sorry.

"Where are you going?"

"That's not important. The important thing is that I won't be near you. You're in danger as long as I want you. As long as I follow you, as long as I have people watching you. In danger. You'll never be safe while I'm here."

Anticipation beats in my chest. Maybe it's wrong to be excited by a man like him. Maybe it's disloyal to be interested in someone else. But Damon is right. He is a riddle I can't solve, and I've had so few of those. He's a warm, breathing puzzle with wooden parts and hidden clasps.

I still remember the boy he was, so fierce and alone.

What would I want with a puny kid?

He said that to me so I wouldn't be afraid of him. It worked.

It worked too well, because even knowing what he's become, what he's capable of, I'm not afraid when he's near me. My body feels electric, my breath comes short, but not from fear.

I place my hand on his arm. The first touch. Heat arcs from him to me, along with a jolt of boldness. "What would you want with a puny kid?" I ask him.

The corner of his mouth turns up. "You're in over your head."

Dark water. Sharp rocks. I lift my chin, determined not to let him bring me low. "That's probably true, but I know a secret. You are, too."

He moves so quickly I can't anticipate, can't defend against it. Suddenly I'm up against the bricks, the coolness against my back, his hard chest an inch from mine.

"My sweet Penny. So smart. So pretty. So fucking little. And you're right." His words are low, bouncing off the bricks as if they're coming from the night itself. "I lived so long underwater that I became a part of it. I rule this place."

"Then what are you afraid of?" I ask softly, knowing it's true.

Because the body in front of me, the arms that hold me in. They're flesh and blood.

"You," he says.

It doesn't seem possible. I'm a poor village girl. He's the prince. How could I pose any danger to him? But when he lowers his head, it feels almost against his will. As if he's being moved by some unknown force, denial and frustration in the air. His lips brush my cheek, barely a soft touch. Chaste. Innocent. Earth shattering.

"It doesn't matter, even if you give Daddy an extension. He has other debts. And he wants me to do this big poker game with him. He says—"

"Wait. *The* big poker game? How did he even get the buy-in money?"

I look away, my cheeks turning hot. My insides a terrible churn.

"Let me guess," he says, his voice dark. Something moves in his eyes, a shadow beneath the waters. "He's going to use you."

It's hard for me to say *yes*. Hard for me to look Damon Scott in the eye now that he knows. Impossible for me to reconcile the daddy who loves me with one who would do this. "He thinks we'll win."

"You won't. And it's not worth the risk. Do you know who's running that game?"

"He came to the diner."

A sharp breath. "After I did?"

"Yes."

"What did he do to you?" His gaze sweeps over me as if he can see beneath my dress. "Are you hurt? Have you seen a doctor?"

"He didn't touch me."

"You're lying."

I spread my hands palm up, as if that proves something. "He came and ordered a slice of pie." I shrug, not wanting to add about the coffee. Or the hundred-dollar bill. "I recognized him right away. I'm pretty sure he didn't recognize me from that day on the playground."

"Good," Damon says tightly. "Stay away from him."

I had given up more dignity in those fifteen minutes than actual sex would have been. Preparing his coffee and fetching pie he had no interest in eating. Only so he could watch me. I had known it was wrong, but I hadn't known how to stop it. *Never again.*

"If I do the game I don't have a choice," I say, "but either way you don't control me."

"About this I do."

I don't know where the impulse comes from, but challenge sparks in the air like electricity. A touch, not with skin but with energy. I can feel him pulsing five feet away from me. "Or what?" I ask softly.

His black eyes narrow. "You want trouble, baby genius? Is that what you're after? Because I know a way you can get a little adventure and help me find my father."

"What are you talking about?"

"I've been looking for him for years. Didn't you know that? Trying to trap him. To hunt him down like the fucking animal that he is."

"For what he did to you."

"For what he did to everyone," Damon says, his voice scathing.

He doesn't need to spell it out. "And you want me as bait."

He looks almost sad. "You always were smart."

So smart that I had to hide for years. It might seem like a small thing. Only numbers. *Only breathing.* I've been in shadows forever, my skin pale, my eyes hungry for the sun. "I'll do it."

He runs a hand through his hair, mussing the silky strands. "No. Forget I said that."

"I can't forget. This is too important."

"It's not safe for you, not if my father has his eye on you."

"He had his eye on me ten years ago," I remind him. "I got away that time."

"Only because—" Damon's voice cuts off, but I can hear the rest. Only because he protected me. Only because he sacrificed himself. He wouldn't do that again. Why would he? "I can't risk it again."

That solidifies my decision. All of us need justice—especially Damon. A sense of protectiveness rises up inside me, as foreign as the possessiveness I feel for him. I don't understand it, but I know he's hurting. I know this will help.

And my life isn't his to risk. It's mine. "I didn't sell myself to your father, but that doesn't mean you own me. That's what I came here to tell you. I'm making the decision to do this."

His eyes turn liquid black. "And what if I decide to stop you?"

"Can you?" I ask, feeling bold now. Feeling free. "He already knows where I work. Already came to see me once. He'll do it again. You know that as well as I do."

"I could keep you here."

I look around at this beautiful prison, the bars

made of ancient oak. He's the one trapped here. Trapped by his anger and his need for revenge. In a perverse way, trapped by me.

"No," I say softly. "I don't think you'll do that."

He smiles, which only makes him seem darker. More dangerous. "That sounds like a challenge."

The idea forms with a sense of deep satisfaction, of rightness.

Damon Scott ties me into knots. The things I feel for him crisscrossing and turned over— sympathy and guilt and longing. And an unbearable anger that he became this man. Not exactly his father, but still so far away from my wild boy.

Everything may have led me to this moment, but not so that I could lose to him.

So that I could beat him.

"Do you want to be challenged, Damon?"

His name hangs in the air, far too intimate for the two of us.

"God yes," he says, and it sounds like a prayer.

"Then let's play cards. If I win then I help you catch Jonathan Scott. I'm your bait."

He looks dubious. "Have you even played much cards?"

"No. Actually never," I admit, feeling shy.

"But I've seen Daddy play plenty."

"Christ." He shakes his head, at once amused and dismissive. "And when I win, what will you give me? I think you know the answer to that. You'll stay here with me. You'll be mine. Mine to keep, Penny. Mine to protect."

CHAPTER TWELVE

OF COURSE WE don't play cards at anything as mundane as a kitchen table.

Not over a coffee table, the way Daddy sometimes fiddles with an old deck, shuffling the cards and running them through his fingers. He would never even bother with Solitaire. It couldn't satisfy that itch.

Damon has a private card table, deep emerald velvet and butter-soft leather on the bumper surrounding. There are only two seats at the table, even though poker usually has more. I imagine private business meetings happening in this small wood-lined room.

Or maybe he brings women here.

It seems appropriate for a man like him. A bordello for people turned on by risk.

He pulls out a chair for me, every inch the gentleman. Even in a shirt soft from wear, in slacks less than crisp, he could be in a magazine for menswear. His eyebrow rises as I stare at him. My distrust of him must be plain on my face, because he seems pleased.

"Thanks," I mutter, dropping into the most magical chair I've ever sat in.

I turn my face away so I can hide the look of pure bliss I must have. God, I would sleep in this chair. I would live in it. The thick leather cushions cradle my body like a cloud.

"Comfortable?" he asks casually, laughter in his voice. He knows. Of course he does.

He sits across from me, all business. "How many cards?"

Now I see the point of the chairs. They're a distraction, like his movie star smile. Keeping me from seeing what's underneath. "What game do you play?"

He smiles. "I play all of them, baby. I want to know which one you like."

Awareness rushes over my skin, smooth as water down my arms, my back. I can't help the shiver that comes, his words a sensual caress. "Five," I tell him, my voice faint.

"A classic," he says, sounding pleased.

Of course I immediately regret the decision. Anything that makes him happy must be bad.

He pulls a fresh deck from a little shelf under the table, the plastic wrapper glinting off the lamp overhead. His hands are strong but deft, tugging the little blue strip with practiced ease. The wrapper comes off, discarded into a small leather wastebin.

The scent of new paper and whatever glue coats the cards fills the small space as he pulls out the deck. His hands move impossibly fast, shuffling the cards with intimate knowledge. The same intimate knowledge I imagine he has with women.

You're a woman, my mind helpfully supplies.

Damon Scott won't be intimate with any part of my body. Not if I win this game.

There's a sense of loss about that, but also power—because I'll be the one to decide my fate.

He deals the cards so fast they look like blades through the air, flying into two neat piles in front of us. I stare at the classic red designs, the nondescript backs hiding their numbers and their suits, my stomach as small and hard as a rock. How did I get here so fast?

"Shouldn't we have chips?" I ask, because I'd like to count something right now.

"I don't think we need them," he says, his voice smooth and certain. "We won't play long enough for that. One hand should do it, I think."

The knot in my throat makes it hard to swallow. "One hand?"

He smiles that stupid-beautiful smile. "Luck of the draw."

One hand means I won't be able to count the cards. There's only what I have. Not enough to be statistically significant. Does he know that I can count cards? I was sure he wouldn't know. Being able to do advanced calculus in theory doesn't mean you have perfect recall.

Or maybe his insistence on one hand has nothing to do with counting.

Maybe he doesn't want to waste time before claiming me.

My gaze somehow strays to his throat, to the place at the collar of his shirt, tanned skin and a hint of dark hair. Such a personal detail to show in public. Then again we're not in public. No, this is very private. Enough to make my breath come faster.

"Fine," I say, wanting this to be over more than I want to win.

No, I can still do this. My odds are as good as his—better, because I can at least count what I see.

"Aces high or low," he adds. "No wild cards."

I pick up my cards and look at them. A pair of jacks. Not the worst hand. Not the best.

The other three cards are all spades, which is

exciting in another way. If I were to turn in my jacks, I might get back two spades. And that would be a strong hand. Probably a winning one.

Damon lifts only the corner of his cards, glancing at them briefly before pushing them back down on the table. It's the kind of move only an experienced player could do, whereas I'm holding mine upright, my hands almost trembling. I push them down onto the table, clumsy.

He leans forward, his dark eyes large in the dim light. "Now that we've seen our cards, we could up our bet. Do you want to call, baby genius?"

The nickname plants itself inside me, some deep buried seed that finds new life. "Don't call me that. And I thought you were already taking everything, if you win. What else could I give you?"

"A kiss," he says, seeming contented as if he's already won. "And it wouldn't be something I would take. You would give it to me."

I stare at him, more shocked than I should be. Sex. I had offered him *sex,* and he turned me down. Because he isn't like his father. And I suppose that's still true. I doubt Jonathan Scott would ever ask for a kiss.

Somehow I could keep a serious face when we

were talking about sex, but the suggestion of a kiss brings heat to my cheeks. "You want me to kiss you?"

"Anywhere you like."

"Your cheek," I say immediately, but it doesn't feel as innocent as I meant it. Not when I imagine that dark stubble against my lips, the scent of him up close, the taste of his skin burrowing deep.

He laughs, enjoying himself more than is decent. Really, nothing about him is decent. "Your choice. And if you're calling the bet, that means I have to put something more in. What would you like?"

Definitely not a kiss, even if my imagination whispers that I might like it. "My father's debt."

"Ten thousand dollars for a kiss," he says, his voice thoughtful.

My chest burns at the implication that I'm for sale. That even if I were for sale, that I'd be worth that much. I feel more like an object than a person. Except I'm not the one who started me down this path. Damon did that himself, when he proposed taking me instead of Daddy's debt.

You know that Daddy is the reason you're in this mess.

My mind needs to be quiet sometimes.

"Take it or leave it," I say, sounding unconcerned.

He makes a sound, kind of tortured, like I just said something sexy. I didn't say anything provocative, at least I didn't think so, but he seems to like it when I challenge him. It's enough to make me want to stop... but not really, because I'm going to fight to my last breath.

"Take it," he says, sounding almost cheerful as he pushes in his entire hand.

My breath catches. "All of them?"

That means he has a terrible hand. It also means that he could have *anything* on the next round. Most people think of randomness as favoring chaos. That he wouldn't be likely to get something strong in a single hand. But really the odds are about the same to get a strong hand as a weak.

"Every last one."

True randomness doesn't play favorites.

It's just as likely to give you fifty heads in a row than an equal split of heads and tails. Then again we don't have a truly random sample, not with us holding ten out of fifty-two cards. Whatever he picks up won't be any of these. I bite my lip, running through numbers in my head, determined to make use of what little data I have, running simulations in these precious few seconds.

"God, you're incredible," he says, sounding reverent.

Only then do I realize I'd been lost in thought.

And he's staring at me, intent and for once serious. Brennan had looked at me that way and called me pretty. Damon looked at me like I was some other creature, more than a human—a goddess.

"Three for me," I say, taking the safer bet. That means keeping my jacks and pushing the rest back. Giving up any chance of a flush, because then I could end up with nothing at all.

Damon deals the cards with swift utility, the same way Brennan looks when he uses a wrench. It's simply a tool, one he's deeply familiar with. One he uses on a daily basis.

Only then do I realize my fatal flaw. No matter how many numbers I have, Damon has something stronger. He has a lifetime of experience. Of knowledge and instinct. The subconscious mind can filter far more information than we fully understand. He can make a call based on his gut.

Then again I'm not sure what possible instinct

could make him send all the cards back.

I pick up my three new cards, along with my original two.

The first two dealt are spades, exactly what I would have needed to complete a flush. No additional pairs or jacks, which means I'm left with my original single pair.

My heart sinks. I struggle to keep my expression blank, not to reveal anything even though this is the only hand we'll play. It seems important that he not know my weakness, whether I win or lose.

Oh God, what if I lose? What reckless impulse possessed me to agree to this game?

Actually you're the one who suggested it.

"What do you have?" Damon asks, all politeness now.

"You first," I say, pushing off reckoning as long as possible.

If he has three of a kind or a straight, I'll never forgive myself. I could have had more, if only I had risked more. Is this how Daddy gets in deep, always chasing a bigger pot, hating himself when he plays safe?

Damon turns over his cards one by one. An ace of hearts. A queen of clubs. A ten of hearts. A three of spades. So far the cards make nothing, but if he has an ace or a queen in his hand I'm done.

I'll be sleeping in this house tonight. Maybe even in his bed.

Bile rises in my throat, because it doesn't matter how handsome his face or how strong his body. Ownership would be the ultimate loss. It doesn't matter if he brings my body pleasure, not if my mind's trapped in a cage.

He flips the card. *A ten.*

The breath I'm holding rushes out. "Oh, thank God."

His expression is even as he says. "Let's see them, baby."

With shaking hands I let the cards tumble over, all at once. My pair of jacks beats the tens, but not by much. Everything feels over sharp, the quiet hum of the house outrageously loud. Adrenaline, I realize. This is the rush. This is why Damon plays the game. Why he loves it, even when he loses.

He curses softly. "Call me the moment you see him. Don't serve him coffee. Don't bring him pie. Don't do a damn thing but pick up the phone and call me when he comes back."

CHAPTER THIRTEEN

IT'S ON THE next Thursday night that I hear it—the tumble of a pebble on cement.

Someone's following me in the darkness, the streetlamps busted long ago. It's a strange feeling to wish to be mugged. To long for a faceless villain in a city full of them.

Anyone but Jonathan Scott.

I'm halfway between the diner and home. I weigh the options between one breath and the next. The diner is more public, more lighted, more known. But the apartment has a lock.

Footsteps echo mine, and I know he's getting closer.

I move faster over the broken sidewalk, keeping my head low as if I'm in a storm. It rained earlier that night, but it had cleared up. There's no storm except inside my mind.

Don't fight them. It only makes it worse.

A shiver takes my whole body, despite the muggy night air.

The devil himself is behind me. Even if he'll

catch me, I have to fight. I have to run. I sprint down the sidewalk, not even pretending anymore. I don't think he's close, not when I reach my building, but it doesn't matter. He must know where I live.

I reach my apartment and slam the door, relieved to have made it in time.

In the kitchen I grab the cream-colored phone with its tangled spiral cord. The number comes to me by heart. I only had to see it once to remember it forever.

He answers on the second ring. "Penny?"

"He's here." Only then do I realize I'm out of breath, my lungs burning. "He followed me home."

"In your apartment?"

"No," I say on a harsh breath.

A knock comes at the door, loud and hard enough to shake the walls.

"Oh no," I whisper.

"Stay there," Damon says, his voice as sharp as a blade. "Wait for me. I'm coming."

Daddy blinks at me from his recliner, clearly woken from a nap. His eyes are cloudy, as if he took the pain meds for his knee. As if he took too many pain meds. "Who is it?"

I don't know whether he means the door or

the phone. I shake my head, clinging to the receiver with both hands. "How far are you?" I whisper.

He swears. "Farther than I should be. He must have planned this. He left breadcrumbs out of the city."

"You're not close," I say, the note of finality harsh to my own ears.

Damon says more about how he's on his way, about holding on. It all mixes with the chaos in my head, the sound of rising water, the sound of currents swirling around me. The line goes dead. There's no help. No time.

Another knock, at almost the exact same volume.

"Penny?" Daddy says, his face gone pale.

"It's Jonathan Scott."

Surprise flickers across his face. "He's here?"

Blood pumps through my veins. My body fights what's happening as much as my mind.

Don't fight them. Except I can't seem to stop.

"Open it," Daddy says, his voice fearful now. "It will be worse if we don't."

I leave the chain in place while I open the door, a feeble defense. A sliver of Jonathan Scott appears, as slick and as smooth as ever. "You," I say, surprised my voice doesn't tremble.

"Me. May I come inside?" It's not really a question.

"Who are you?" I say, because I'm stalling. I want Damon to magically appear in the dimly lit hallway, but he won't. He won't make it in time. What will happen without him?

What will happen to bait when the trap doesn't work? It gets eaten.

"The owner of this building."

I swallow hard. He's the owner? Which means that he already has access to my apartment. He can come inside. He can burn the place down for all that the law can touch him.

"You're not the super," I say, still stalling.

"He works for me."

The super is a disgusting human being, which suits this place perfectly. *Hurry, Damon.* "How do I know I can trust you?"

I can't, I can't, I can't.

He smiles. "You definitely can't trust me. Run and tell your daddy that Jonathan Scott is here."

I slam the door shut, staring at the peeling white paint on the door, the rusted metal chain. "Oh God," I whisper. "What do we do?"

There's a brief but potent fantasy where I fling myself out of the window. Three stories down. That would be enough to end things, wouldn't it?

That would be enough to save me?

Bodies want to go on living, no matter what happens to them.

It only makes it worse.

"Open the door," Daddy says, his voice panicked.

"Help is on the way. We just have to let this play out." I take deep breaths. My voice comes out even. Only my blurring vision gives any hint to the turmoil inside. "Everything will be fine."

It doesn't even sound like a lie.

A sound of an animal in pain fills the room. It's coming from Daddy. *Not me, not me.* "I'm sorry, Penny. I'm so sorry. I didn't mean for this to happen. I didn't think he'd come here."

There's a wrench in my chest. A horrible turn of grief already tight. "What did you do?"

"I entered the poker game."

I'm not even a person anymore. Not flesh and blood. None of the soft curves the men would want. I'm clockwork, made of metal and wood. Unfeeling. Unflinching in the face of familial betrayal. "How is that possible? How could you do that without my permission?"

How could I mean so little to you?

That's not what I'm asking. I want to know the mechanics of it.

Which gears turned to make this beating heart.

He uses his damp T-shirt to wipe his forehead. "I told them you agreed."

"And if I open the door and tell him I refuse?"

His face turns pale. "Then I'd have broken my word to Jonathan Scott."

And we both know what that would mean. Death. A particularly painful one.

The irony is that I would probably still be part of the pot. That's the merciless version of justice he used to rule the streets. It would mean the end of us both. Mutually assured destruction. Neither of us have a choice now.

Then I'm opening the door, inviting the devil inside. "Come in."

He stalks into the apartment as if he owns it, which he does. His cool grey gaze takes in my father and his broken knee with a single, disdainful glance.

Daddy struggles to stand. And fails. "Mr. Scott," he says. "What can we do for you?"

What a sad attempt at valiance. That makes my heart squeeze in a way his apology never could. Who am I to blame my father for his addictions? He couldn't control them anymore than I could make my brain into something else.

Jonathan Scott gestures to the lumpy armchair as if it's a gold-plated antique in his palace. "Please sit down, George. Don't strain yourself on my account."

Daddy shudders a little, his good leg already failing him. I move quickly to help him. There's no point in overexerting himself. Nothing he does would stop this.

Jonathan Scott takes the maroon corduroy sofa. Somehow his presence makes it seem like a throne. "I understand my son has been to visit you."

My heart stops. Damon Scott was here, in our apartment? Daddy didn't tell me that. Was that before or after I went to the Den? He might see it as a kindness to harass my father instead of me.

"I told him we'd get it," Daddy says, breathing hard. "I swear."

"Don't lie to me," Jonathan Scott says, his voice underlaid with steel. "There's no way for you to get ten thousand dollars. Little Penny could serve a hundred pies a day, and you'd never be able to pay."

I've had enough.

"Stop it," I say, because I'm the reason he's really here. "Leave him alone."

A flash of excitement crosses Jonathan Scott's

face, sending a shiver down my spine. He likes it when I talk back, when I fight. That's what Jessica told me, but I told her the truth. I don't think I can let him. Like I'm underwater. The body will fight to breathe.

His voice is mild. "I could. Leave him alone, I mean. If you want me to."

It was always leading to this. I try to keep my voice steady. "What do you mean?"

"Ten thousand dollars." He pulls out a thick envelope. I can guess what's inside. Money. It's his gamble. In this rundown tenement, his odds are good. "Would you like this, Penny?"

"No, leave her out of this," Daddy says. "She didn't have nothing to do with it."

"You'll have to give the money to Damon yourself," Jonathan Scott says to Daddy, his dark liquid gaze still trained on me. "Do you think you could manage that? Or would you gamble again, hoping to turn it into twenty or thirty thousand?"

We may not need to give that money to Damon Scott, but Daddy doesn't know that. It still hurts to think he might trade my life for one last gamble. Then again isn't that what he always does?

"I'll make sure he gets it," I say, imagining myself waiting in the apartment for him. How safe I would be. It's enough to make me laugh, if I was capable of smiling. What an illusion, safety. The impressive thing isn't what I can do with numbers, with lines and curves in my head. The impressive thing is that I ever believed, even for one moment, that home would be safe.

"You won't," Jonathan Scott says, casual in his dismissal.

"Why not?" I say, almost a whisper.

"You'll be with me."

With him, where Damon can find me. Where Damon can save me.

At least I hope so.

"No!" Daddy fights to stand. And fails. "You can't do this."

Jonathan Scott gives me a smile that's almost handsome. If I didn't know how evil he was I could have been fooled. It's enough to prove he doesn't have to force girls. With his smooth silver fox looks and his money he could have anyone he wanted. He prefers to force.

"It's up to you," he says.

"You're a monster," I tell him, this one statement sincere.

"That's right," he murmurs. "Fight me."

Don't fight them. I'm shaking with something—maybe fear, maybe anger. I prefer to be angry. Some part of me thinks it might seem more realistic, but the truth is I *am* angry. It's not pretend. "How dare you do this?"

"Offer you money? Well, sure, call the cops. Tell them how horrible I am for paying your daddy's debts."

"Aren't the police in your pockets?" I ask bitterly.

"Or you can take your chances with Damon Scott. He has quite a reputation." He glances at Daddy's broken leg. "I suppose you're already familiar with it. What did he promise to take next?"

Daddy looks at me, his eyes helpless. It doesn't matter who broke his knee. Doesn't matter that the debt to Damon Scott has been won, because that was the deal I made. To be bait for this man. This dark king.

"Tick tock," the king says. "Would you like the money?"

He shifts ever so slightly on the old lumpy sofa, revealing a flash of silver in his coat. A gun. Will he use it if I refuse him? It doesn't matter, because this is my purpose.

"I'll do it."

In a graceful move he stands and strides from the room, leaving the money on the sofa. It's too much to hope that he's changed his mind as soon as I've agreed. No, he expects me to follow him. I'm not even worth a basic command. I'm a dog, trained to heel by poverty, trained to obey by circumstances.

"Wait," I call after him into the hallway. "I'm coming."

There are only minutes to run back, to hold Daddy's trembling hand. To squeeze.

"Damon Scott will come," I whisper, breathless. "I'll try to leave a trail. Tell him to follow me. Tell him what happened."

His eyes are wide, helpless. I don't even know if he's hearing me.

I grasp a handful of coins from my tip jar, mostly pennies left after digging out the quarters and dimes to spend. A few nickels. And that's what I need—dark copper pennies made green and blackened from use.

I run down the stairs, the coins clutched in my sweaty palm. It's only on the street that he stops, as motionless and contained as if he had been standing there all along. I'm out of breath, still wearing my old diner uniform. A handful of loose change he can't see.

"I don't wait for you, little girl. That's not how this works."

Go to hell. That probably isn't going to help my position any.

And that's not what I really want to say. *Please find me, Damon.* He's the only one who can solve this for me. He's also the reason I'm in the middle of this, a twisted game of tug-of-war between father and son.

"Okay," I say softly. "I'll be good. I swear."

"Do you really think Daddy is going to use the money to pay off the debt?"

I don't care about the debt anymore. Don't care about the money. What I care about is that Daddy tells Damon Scott what happened. "He knows what I'm giving up."

Silver eyes gleam in the dark. "Do you?"

I glare at him. "You want to have sex with me."

"Wrong."

Goose bumps rise on my skin, despite the warm night. *It only makes it worse.* "What, then?"

"I want to break you down into parts—into hope and despair. Into love and fear. I want to consume your humanity, feast on you, until there's nothing left but a small, jagged core at the center."

What a bastard. "Why?"

He laughs. "Do you ever think about how

mechanical sex is? Men so desperate for something warm and wet to fuck. A purely physical sensation. We might as well be automatons."

I've never thought about sex like that. I never think about it at all.

That's a lie, Penny. You think about Damon.

He continues, his expression severe. "I learned to block out physical sensations as a child. Pain. Sex. Hunger. They only touch our bodies. Not our minds."

I swallow hard, remembering how that wild boy had left home. Something had been done to him. And something had been done to the man in front of me. Men turned into monsters. "What happened to you?"

He holds his hand out like I'm a little girl crossing the street. "Come along."

"You're insane."

"No, little peach. I'm the only sane one in a world full of rabid animals."

Please find me, Damon. Find me in time. I put my empty hand in his. He squeezes gently, as if to comfort me. It's a strange sensation, to be consoled by my enemy. Less strange to be led by the king. I drop a single penny near the curb, hoping it will be small enough to escape notice, hoping it will shine enough to bring Damon to me.

He takes me down two streets with a familiarity that shows he's used to walking the west side streets. Every few steps I drop a penny, leaving a trail for him to follow.

As long as he comes in time. *Please, Damon.*

The sign for the Midtown Asylum has long since crumbled, leaving only a large, plantation-style building. On either side, there are houses falling down. It's dark inside them. Empty.

We're alone. The last coin falls into the overgrown weeds.

He unlocks the front door and steps inside, finally releasing me.

Leaving me to stare at the pictures spread over the floor. The insides of senators' houses. The interiors of city hall. Windows into our twisted little world.

"The desk," he says, hanging his coat on a hook like this is a five-star hotel instead of a broken down mental hospital.

I take a step forward, horrified to find my bedroom in a photo. "You watched me."

My faded quilt and my kitten poster. The room I had undressed in and slept in. The bed where I had touched myself thinking of Damon Scott.

As if he can read my thoughts he smiles. "Sometimes at night, I'd hear you breathe faster. See your hand moving under the covers. It's so beautiful, the way you love yourself."

My eyes widen. "I'm not leaving here, am I?"

"Not alive." He sounds almost regretful about that.

The last thing I see will be those silver eyes. I run for the door, knowing I'm trapped.

Of course he catches me.

That night I learn why Damon Scott could hold his breath underwater for so long. Because his father forced him there, longer and longer until he had to adapt to survive. It's a brutal existence, the water closing in on you, almost praying for death because it would be a relief. Green tiles. Black water. The certainty that this will be the last thing I see.

The decision to survive, if only to spite the monster.

My body is broken and split apart. Violated. Twisted into something unfeeling.

That night my mind cracks into a million splinters.

But the king was wrong about one thing. I don't die, no matter how many times I wish I would. I learn to hold my breath, the same way

Damon Scott did. We have something in common now. We're both monsters. Not the kind you can see on the outside. He wears a secret smile on his handsome face. Bruises faded back to pale skin on my naked body.

It's only inside that something can never be repaired.

Only inside that I never really leave the water.

Inside that I learn to need the dark.

CHAPTER FOURTEEN

ALL THOSE YEARS ago I didn't like the water. I was too busy clinging to the slippery rubber, too frantic kicking to stay close to Mama. Way too afraid of drifting away.

And then Damon Scott came into my life. A force of nature. A tidal wave. And I learn that there are compensations for drowning. That I can float, my body shivering and catatonic.

My mind can float, too.

That's how Damon finds me.

He pulls my body from the water, his hands iron-hard on my bruised skin. Strong arms cradle my limp body. Held so close I could hear his heart beating, too fast. I want to tell him—don't worry. I'm okay here, floating down the river in my head.

Except I can't say a word. That's one thing about floating.

I hear him talking to me, his low voice so different than ever before. He's been amused and casually cruel. Never terrified and tense, never broken.

The words come through a thick swirl of dark water, my thoughts inky black.

"Wake up, sweetheart. Talk to me. Oh God, what did he do to you? Tell me where you're hurt. Let me help you." He speaks faster the longer he goes, his voice turning hoarse. "Beautiful girl. Smart girl. Come back to me."

He carries me for what feels like miles, my uniform drenched, his grip impossibly tight.

Part of me wonders how we must look, a man in a suit carrying a half-conscious girl. Does no one stop him? Does no one wonder? The irony is that he's the only man who would protect me.

"I'm sorry," he whispers against my forehead. "God, I'm so sorry. I tried to stay away from you. I wanted to keep you safe. If he knew… if he touched you…"

Jonathan Scott did more than touch me. He tortured me. He violated me in every way that a man can hurt a woman. I'm sure there's tearing, enough to show what's happened. I wish there weren't any marks, not because it would hurt me less, but because it would hurt *him* less.

The unlikely prince come to take me away.

No white horse, though. Only his bespoke Italian loafers against the asphalt. It takes me a moment to realize that it's raining, the water on my skin fresh and clean. Unlike that horrible pool of water where I had been trapped, unlike the salty tears I couldn't hold in.

Damon swears, but I wish I could tell him the rain will help. I don't want to be dirty.

We reach a building in the historic district, with white stone and black metal balconies on each window. He pushes inside as if he owns the place, and maybe he does. Maybe he owns the entire street.

I hear a feminine gasp. "Is she—"

Is she dead? That's what the unknown woman asks.

The strange part is not knowing the answer. Am I dead?

"She'll wish she was," Damon says, his voice hard.

It sounds like a threat, but I feel the tension in his body. He's worried about me. About what happened before he showed up. Before Jonathan Scott shoved me into a black pool of water and closed a grate on top of me, trapping me inside. Before he held me down and—

My mind shies away from the truth.

Maybe I would wish I were dead, by the time this is over.

"What can I do?" the woman asks.

It makes me wonder if she's Damon's girl-friend. His lover. His prostitute? I don't know how he deals with women, except to pay them. She must be close to him if she was in his house.

"Blankets," he says. "Every single one you can find."

That sounds practical, but I don't feel cold. I don't feel anything, really.

Damon carries me upstairs and lays me down on a large bed. *His bed?*

He pulls back the covers, settling my wet body into the middle. Part of me recognizes that it must be comfortable—the way I sink into the mattress, the velvet drapes hanging from a thickly carved bedframe. I'm disconnected from my body, though. As if it sank to the bottom of the water, landing on hard rocks.

And my mind kept floating along.

"Damon," I whisper, surprised to find my lips cracked and hard. How can they be dry after almost drowning? Everything feels upside down, inside out.

His eyes look pure black. "I'm here."

"Don't leave," I whisper, swallowing hard to get the words out. "Please."

"Not yet." It's a promise, both to stay and to

go. I have him for now, which is more than I ever thought I would have. More than a peasant girl deserves with a prince.

"I'm sorry."

He swears. "Don't."

"You found them. Tell me you found them—"

"Yes, your breadcrumbs. My smart girl. My beautiful girl." He presses a kiss to my forehead. I know his lips are touching my skin. Some part of me registers that fact. But I don't *feel* anything. Not pleasure. Not fear. When he brushed his knuckles against my cheek at the diner I'd felt the echo of his touch for days. And now I can't feel anything.

The woman comes into the room with an armful of quilts and blankets. She's older than me but not by much. Very beautiful. It wouldn't surprise me if they were together, but she doesn't look jealous. She looks worried, about me.

Damon reaches to the neckline of my uniform. There's no warning before he rips it away.

I should feel something. Embarrassment as I'm exposed, naked and bruised. At least I should feel cold as the air touches my damp skin. I'm still separate from my body, unable to feel a thing.

"What are you doing?" the woman asks, concern plain in her soft voice.

Damon gives her a hard look. "Fucking her limp body. What do you think?"

It's the same voice he used years ago. *What would I want with a puny kid?*

And then he unclasps his belt. It makes a whip-like sound through the air as he pulls it off. The old me would have flinched at the sound. Now I just stare, unblinking, unfeeling.

"I can do it," the woman says, moving as if to undress.

A cold laugh. "As much as I'd love to see the two of you in bed together, I don't want to see what happens when Gabriel finds out I saw you naked."

"You saw me naked at the auction," she says.

"That doesn't count. You weren't his then."

So they aren't together. I can't even feel relief, not with the word *auction* hanging in the air. Is that what would have happened to me? And as horrible as that sounds, wouldn't that have been better than this?

Anything would be better than this.

Damon pushes the damp white fabric from his shoulders, revealing hard packed muscle and lines of ink. I hadn't expected to see tattoos beneath that expensive suit fabric. None of it peeks out onto his hands or neck. It's all perfectly contained to his chest, his abs. Ancient scrollwork and dragon scales over a modern man.

What's the point of getting such beautiful artwork on skin no one can see?

"I'll go find Anders," the woman says.

Damon's voice is a drawl, closer as the bed dips in his direction. "Really intent on making this a threesome, aren't you?"

"He's a doctor."

"He lost his license," Damon says, his touch burning hot as he pulls me into his arms. Oh God, I didn't feel anything. I didn't *want* to feel anything, but he's like a flame. I'm consumed by him.

I want the girl to be worried about me now, to help me get away from this.

To pull me out of the fire, but she seems content to leave me there, especially as Damon smooths a wet lock of hair away from my cheek. He probably looks gentle, but she can't see how it burns.

Only Damon's eyes are cold, black stones that give nothing away.

"Gabriel said it was fine," she says. "Anders stitched his gunshot wound."

Damon glances at her. "Gabriel was shot?"

"Grazed. On his neck. The bullet was meant

for me."

"You don't know that," says a new voice, male and gravelly.

The girl sounds surprised. "You shouldn't be standing."

"And you shouldn't be in Damon's bedroom."

"This is his bedroom?" she asks, uncertain.

So this is his bed. And this is his house.

Of course it is. Expensive and luxurious and completely impersonal.

It doesn't mean anything that he brought me here, that he holds me tight as if he can't stand to let go. I tell myself that, but it still burns too hot. His arms and his abs. He's hard and warm and painful.

And then I feel something against my hip. Oh God.

I may not have gone all the way with Brennan but I recognize that. This one's bigger and more insistent. When I try to squirm away Damon holds me tighter.

"I heard you almost died," Damon says, his voice casual, as if he's not throbbing against me. "Did you lose…what? A whole teaspoon of blood?"

The man responds with equal languor. "A

quarter cup, at least. We should talk."

I can already hear the words. They whip around in the water between us. Words about Jonathan Scott and about pain. About bullets and about sex.

"You can talk in front of me," the woman says. "I want to know."

No, you don't. I want to tell her that.

Damon looks at me, reading the truth in my eyes. "In private," he says.

She doesn't give up. "Why? What happened to her? Does it have to do with your father?"

Only when Damon pulls away from me do I feel the cold. It's deep in my bones, settled like ice that will never melt. I want the fire back, but I know it will hurt. It doesn't matter what I want. Damon is already getting dressed, already leaving. Already riding away on his invisible white horse.

"Stay with her," he tells the girl. "Her name's Penny."

"What happened to her?" the woman says again, her voice desolate, knowing he won't answer.

Of course Damon obliges, leaving without another word. Then it's only this woman and me, someone who was auctioned off like some rare and valuable object, and meanwhile I'm cracked into a thousand pieces like a worthless one. The princess and the pauper.

✧   ✧   ✧

SHE DOESN'T UNDRESS like Damon, which is a small relief. I don't think I could handle any more vulnerability in this night. But she does join me in the bed, stroking my hair gently until I fall asleep.

I wake up with the room darker, the shadows deeper.

Her body feels warm and still beside mine, as if she had drowsed too.

Who is she? And why does she care what happens to me? Or maybe she does whatever Damon tells her to without question. I'm all too familiar with that unblinking obedience.

"Are you one of them?" I ask, half in the dream world.

"One of who?"

The whores. I can't say the word, not only because it would offend her. Because I'm one of them. What are we called, anyway? "One of the girls. The ones Damon collects when someone can't pay the loan back."

"Do you mean the strippers?"

"Are they strippers?" I ask, my voice thick with sleep.

I guess it makes sense. A way to make money where none had been. And probably some of the customers are the very same men who owe money. It's a complete circuit, powering Damon Scott's rise to power.

But I can't really imagine Damon on a cigarette littered floor, tossing dollar bills onstage.

My eyes flutter closed again. "I thought he kept them for himself. I imagined a harem of girls, one for every day of the month."

At least that's how he had made it sound. Was that supposed to make it more palatable?

So I would go more easily into my captivity?

She sounds contemplative, as if she's wondering the same thing. "There aren't other girls. At least not here. What made you think there were?"

Come to terms with what you have to do. "He threatened to take me. If Daddy didn't pay."

"Maybe he wanted you to work off the debt," she says, uncertain.

But I swear to God you'll be mine.

"No," I say, drifting back into sleep. He said he'd make me like it. The strange thing was, I believed him. "He told me what he wanted to do. Him and me."

She holds my hand when the doctor comes.

He doesn't wear a white coat or carry a black

bag. Instead he wears only black slacks, exposing his broad chest with pale red hair and silvery scars I've seen on men who fight a lot. His soft-sided grey cooler looks more like it should carry body parts rather than heal them.

"Trust him," she whispers, squeezing my hand.

I close my eyes, holding onto her when he examines me.

The doctor may look like a thug but his manner is professional. Impersonal, even. He doesn't express any surprise over finding my ribs bruised or my rectum torn. It's with a fast, impersonal touch that he cleans my wounds and applies topical antibiotics.

And blissfully he has pain medicine. Serious, hardcore pain medicine. The kind you can get addicted to. That's what I need right now. I need to escape my own mind, my memories. I need oblivion.

The pain medicine backfires, because I can't wake up. Not even when I want to.

In the darkness of my nightmares Damon can't reach me. I'm deep underneath the water, where it's only black. And on the surface, a thick layer of ice. I don't know if he could have made me like kissing, if I would have ever liked sex, but there's only fear now.

Only a cold certainty that whatever comes next will hurt.

Only the strange dread that I'll like it that way.

✧   ✧   ✧

THE NEXT MORNING I wake up encased in ice, the events of last night frozen away. And I'm sure I can stay this way, as long as I don't talk or move or think. I stare up at the blank ceiling, carefully not imagining about Damon sleeping in this same place night after night.

Avery is the young woman's name. She stays by my side the whole night, only leaving briefly to confer with the doctor and someone who brings clothes for us both.

She dresses me in a loose tank top and yoga pants.

On an intellectual level I know the clothes are comfortable. They feel like velvet against my skin. Apparently rich people even have different workout clothes.

But on a physical level I don't feel anything. Not pain.

Definitely not hunger, especially once I see the table heavy with food.

Damon sits with another man at the table, speaking in low tones. Both of them stand when we come into the room. It's an old world courtesy, but one lacking any warmth. Damon's eyes are as cold as I've ever seen them. And they don't linger long on me.

Avery leads me to one of the empty chairs before taking one opposite me.

I stare at the teacup in front of me, only distantly curious. It may as well be a flying saucer. Something to be poked and prodded. Examined. Nothing that could provide comfort.

The whole world seems foreign now.

"Did you find anything?" the other man says. I remember Avery talking to him. *Gabriel.*

There could be a thousand meanings, but I know which one it is. The same way I could count cards and calculate statistics—without really wanting to. Did he find anything in that abandoned mental hospital?

"Nothing useful," Damon answers, his voice low and flat.

Gabriel presses forward. "You know him best. What's his next move?"

"He thinks he's teaching me a lesson. What does any teacher do?"

Reinforce the lesson. Give homework. My mind

flashes to Damon in the old trailer, holding that damned book of trigonometry. My stomach turns over, threatening to spill over the nice shiny china.

"Does that mean Avery is safe?"

A cold smile crosses Damon's handsome face. "The opposite."

Gabriel makes a low growling sound. "Then we can't wait."

"No," Damon says agreeably.

The men will go looking for Jonathan Scott. Will they find him? That seems doubtful. This is an elaborate game. I haven't seen enough of the cards to count them. And I'm only a chip in the pile, moved around on the velvet without a thought.

"So I'll bring Avery back," the other man says.

Damon nods. "We can meet this afternoon."

Avery seems to perk up. "Can you maybe talk *to* me instead of *about* me?"

"I'll bring you back to my house," Gabriel says to her, his expression a strange mix of possession and deference. "And then meet with Damon this afternoon."

"What about Penny?"

Everyone in the room looks at me, the heat from the gazes searing. *Look away, look away.*

"What about her?" Gabriel finally asks.

"Who will take care of her?" Avery demands.

Damon doesn't move a muscle but I feel his fury as if it flickers, his own flame. "I'll find someone," he says, nothing in his voice giving away his anger.

"I'll stay with her," Avery says, though I can hear the uncertainty in her voice.

"Absolutely not," Gabriel says. "My house is the safest place for you, especially when both Damon and I aren't there. The security team is already installed there."

"Then she can come with me." Avery kicks me softly under the table. She wants me to say that I agree with her, but I don't really. I like Avery, but she's probably safer without me. "If it's safer there, then she'll be safer, too."

The force of Damon's discontent takes the air from the room. In the tense silence I imagine a million things he could say. *I'll take care of you, Penny.* The fantasy gets stronger.

"Take her," he says, his voice cold as he stands and tosses down his napkin.

Then he leaves the room, as if he decided on his dinner order instead of my fate.

Avery struggles to meet my eyes, but I can't deal with that. Can't deal with the empathy I would find. Can't deal with the questions she would ask.

"What happened to her?" she asks Gabriel instead, a sweet relief. Someone else to answer her questions. Someone else to field the useless empathy.

"You don't want to know," he says, his voice hard.

"I should know if I'm going to help her."

"I'm not sure there's any help for someone who's been through that."

That almost makes me laugh. Maybe if the ice were a little thinner, I would have. But every second that Damon is away from me, the ice hardens. Every time he pushes me away it gets thicker.

It should be a relief that he doesn't seem to be claiming the debt. That he's giving me time to heal. But he's the only person who really understands what I've been through. Because he went through his own hell, with the very same devil.

"Are you speaking from experience?" Avery says, her innocence heartbreaking.

"I saw a lot of fucked-up shit at the whorehouse growing up. Women raped, hurt. Beaten until they weren't recognizable. And still I never saw anything like this."

She makes a sound of sympathy. For me. For him. "I'm sorry."

"Don't apologize, little virgin. I could have freed you. Never forget that. I could have paid a million dollars and then walked away, never fucking that pretty little cunt." A pause, as if to let the words set in. "He fucked her. And then he drowned her."

A sharp breath. "How did she—"

"Survive? She left a trail of breadcrumbs for him to find. He didn't know if he'd make it in time. He had no idea if he'd find a dead body at the bottom of the pool."

Didn't he? Like that day on the river I don't quite remember being pulled from the pool. I don't remember much of last night except the hard currents, the sharp rocks. The metallic taste of blood in the water. That must have been horrible for Damon, but it's hard to feel sympathy.

Hard to feel anything at all.

"Thank God he didn't." Avery sounds painfully earnest.

"What Jonathan Scott did to her... Most people would rather have died."

I know I should feel something about that. Shame, probably.

But all I keep thinking is, what if I *did* die last night? What if the only parts of me worth saving sank to the bottom of that cold pool? I can be dressed up and fed like a doll, but I'm not a person. I can walk around, my body controlled by the people around me.

What makes me human? What makes me *want* to be human?

It seems like a horrible thing to be, so weak and unwilling.

CHAPTER FIFTEEN

AVERY TUCKS ME in at night, murmuring things about Gabriel's huge house.

"It's very comfortable," she assures me. "And *very* safe."

That last part seems to be the sticking point. Not only because of the threat of Jonathan Scott looming over us all. There must be something less than shiny, something not quite gilded in her past. Because she keeps glancing at the walls, as if something terrifying might jump out of the plaster.

She leaves the bathroom light on for me, the door cracked open an inch.

Then she closes the door, probably going to sleep with Gabriel. She doesn't say, but I saw the way he looked at her. The way she looked at him. The lion to the gazelle. Only this gazelle wants to be eaten.

I hear the footsteps first. My heart is a muscle overworked in the last twenty-four hours, already sore and weak from beating so fast. Now it strains against my ribs, making weak protest.

The doorknob turns, a polished silver handle reflecting the light.

Most likely it's Avery checking on me.

Possibly it's someone out of my nightmares.

Damon Scott slips into the room, as casual as if he were visiting for tea. He's still wearing his shirt and vest. Only his shoes are missing, the sole nod to being in his own home. I suppose that counts for casual with him, those black socks on the plush carpet.

He enters the way I imagine he'd visit a lover. A woman in lace lingerie should be waiting for him, not a broken girl in an oversize T-shirt.

He sits on the edge of the bed, his expression unreadable. "Hello, Penny."

Such a mundane greeting.

I want to do something drastic in response. To scream or tear out my hair. Something to show the utter chaos inside me. He must see it. He must *feel* it, having that monster for a father.

Screaming would require feeling something. I would rather not feel, so I say nothing.

That earns me a small smile. "You've been holding up well."

An iceberg holds up well, floating like a massive rock. *Congratulations,* I tell myself with bitter appreciation. I'm a natural phenomenon. And where I'm made from ice, he's a flame.

Even from two feet away I can feel him burn.

"Would you like to stay at Gabriel's house?"

As if it's a vacation, meant to be enjoyed.

As if I have a choice.

"Why?" I whisper. *Why are you here?*

He raises one eyebrow, pretending not to understand. "Avery's a nice girl."

My very own mermaid with glitter fins and blue-green yarn hair. A consolation prize. I'm not good enough for someone to actually love me, to care about me. That couldn't be more clear.

I speak louder. "Why?"

He doesn't pretend this time. "Do you want me to leave?"

That's not an answer. My lips press together. Already I'm annoyed that he made me talk. Where Avery could stroke my hair like I was a pet, something about Damon's blunt taunting requires a response.

His laugh has everything he used to be— defiant and hungry. It has everything he is now, dark and unrepentant. The wild boy may have been alluring in his subtle strength, but the man has a thousand moving pieces. A puzzle I could never hope to solve.

"You'll be safe at Gabriel's house," he says, his tone final.

He stands, about to leave the room.

There was no reason for him to confirm with me personally. It had already been decided at breakfast. And yet here he is, as beautiful and masculine as I can even imagine, taking my breath away. For what?

And then I know the right question to ask. Not, *why are you here?*

"Why do you care?" I whisper.

He pauses without turning. "Do you know why my father chose you?"

Jonathan Scott had said I was a peach. Ripe. Juicy. I can still hear the smooth slide of his voice. I can still feel the sharp bite of his teeth in my flesh. Every part of me tenses, every muscle in my body taut. It was the right question if he wanted a reaction from me—something desperate or even violent. Something dramatic. I press my nails into my palm, forcing down the bile in my throat.

Then Damon looks back at me, his dark eyes knowing. "Because he knew you meant something to me."

A man who owns half the city. Wealthy. Powerful.

The sound that bursts from me should be a

laugh. Instead it sounds like something cracking. "I thought he would be smarter than that. I don't mean anything to you except ten thousand dollars."

Damon gives me a small smile, a little wry. "Smart people don't always have perspective."

Is that why Damon came to visit me? Because he feels like he owes me something? He doesn't owe me anything. It wasn't him who hurt me. He already sacrificed himself for me once.

I always dreamed of being a mermaid. How they could swim around, without a care for what happened above water. In their own little world. Only now do I understand how constraining it would be, how suffocating it can feel even when you can breathe. Whether the water is dark or light, tinged with blood or sparkling blue, you're trapped inside.

"I'm sorry," I say, though I'm not sure what I'm sorry for.

His grief, even though he doesn't look sorrowful.

He looks hard and glinting, like a diamond. That's the way he stares at me, looking almost angry at my words. "I swear to God, Penny. What I would do to you. If only—"

My breath catches. "If only what?"

"If only you weren't so fucking terrified."

I couldn't argue with that. Terror has sunk so deep in my bones it felt like survival. I wasn't sure what would be left if you tried to strip the fear away. Would there be anything to hold me up? "He said he was leaving my virginity," I say, the memory sore and raw. Festering. "He took me from... From the back. But he said he would leave me innocent for you."

Damon doesn't have any of the surprise that Avery did. None of the pity.

And then he takes a step toward me.

Another one, as if pulled by the invisible string of my pain.

He doesn't stop at the edge of the bed. It's *his* bed, after all. Not my personal island. Not a fortress. He puts one knee on the bed. That's the only warning I get before his body covers mine. Caging me. Before he holds me down with the very heat of his presence.

I put my hands up before I realize what that means—it means I'm touching him. My palms against his broad chest, my hands feeling warm skin and hard muscle. I yank my hands back as if they're scalded.

"You're too young," he murmurs.

There's this heat coming off him, like he's a

fire and I'm thawing out. I know it's not safe, being this close. He could burn me. But there's also a small part of me that feels alive, only when he's here. Only when he's on top of me, his warm breath on my forehead.

"I thought the cops couldn't protect me."

"They can't. But I can."

For half a second—sweet relief. I want his protection, even if it means my ruin.

Except that isn't what he's offering. Isn't what he's demanding.

Realization crashes down on me. He's going to send me far away, into the arctic where my ice can set in. I should be grateful for that, but I can't. The whole world will see me as broken, after what happened to me. God, even I agree. He's the only person in the world who could have seen me as whole.

"Because I'm tainted now," I say, my voice wavery.

"Because you're mine. I told you it would happen. This changed the timetable. Changed the methods. But it could not change that one fact."

It's impossible to argue with that when he's braced above me, when the musk and man scent of him surrounds me, when the same sheets that rubbed over his naked body now embrace me.

"There are marks," I say.

On my body. My soul. He gouged me deep enough that I haven't stopped reeling for hours, for days. I will still feel him in years, if I live that long. On my deathbed there will be Jonathan Scott's teeth marks aching on my skin. With my final breath I'll remember how it felt to drown.

Damon nods, his expression grave. "Let me see."

They're in the secret places in my body, the ones I'm too young to show him.

He doesn't wait for me to obey. Instead he grasps the hem of the extra-large T-shirt, yanking it up until cool air flashes over my stomach. The back of his hand touches my pale skin—an accidental touch, fleeting. I suck in a breath, whether from humiliation or something else I don't know. I'm wearing the panties Avery gave me, white with little pink flowers on them.

The edge of the panties is scalloped, little ruffles over my skin.

And underneath, mottled brown and dark red marks that spread over my ribs.

A hiss of something like pain escapes Damon. He stares with a kind of reluctant fascination, unable to look away from the contrast of white fabric on dark bruises.

"You fought him," Damon says, his eyes meeting mine.

There isn't a question in his voice.

Don't fight them. It only makes it worse. I understand now why Jessica told me that. It makes everything harder. Sharper. Darker. I never wanted to fight, the same way I never wanted to drown. It happened, my body reacting to its environment, animal instinct beating out reason.

The question flickers at the edges of my mind. "Maybe that's when I lost myself. When I really broke. When I lost the numbers in my head."

For the first time since he came into the room he looks surprised. "You didn't lose the numbers, Penny. No one can take them away from you."

Then maybe I gave them up voluntarily. Maybe that's the price I had to pay to survive.

My mind has been blessedly quiet ever since I woke in Damon's arms. It's kept me safe from feeling the horror, the pain, but it's also blocked out the numbers.

Damon reaches to his back pocket. I tense, sure that he's going to pull out something terrible. A knife, like he had as the wild boy. A rope. I don't know where my mind conjures all of these ideas, except that my thoughts all follow a train of violence. He's never hurt me, but he seems too enamored of the bruises to really trust.

In his hand is only a pen, something smooth and cylindrical, no doubt expensive.

He pulls the cap off with his straight white teeth, revealing the shining silver point beneath.

With only a veiled glance at me, he lowers his hand to a bare patch of skin on my left side. There's no bruise here. It somehow escaped the struggle. The pen has been against his body, kept in his pocket, but it still feels cool when it touches my skin.

I try to make out what he could be writing based on feel, but there's a dull throb of pain all over and a numbness from the medication. Noise that drowns out the feeling of his fountain pen.

He pulls down the T-shirt before I can see what he's written. Then he straightens, his knee still pressed between mine, only eight hundred thread count sheets and fine wool slacks between us.

"Go with Avery. Be a good girl for her. She'll take care of you."

The word *until* pulses in the air, asking and asking until I can finally voice the question. "Until when?"

"Until I kill my father, of course."

He's all the way to the door before I ask the

question that's been haunting me since I swirled underneath that pool, since I saw exactly what his father had done to make him able to hold his breath so long. "Why haven't you already?"

He stands in front of the dark walnut door, facing away from me. His body locked into position like a statue. His voice almost separate from him, an unknown force in the room.

"That's what he wants. To turn me into a killer. To make me like him."

Finally I understand that though he's been abused and harmed and corrupted in infinite ways, there was one piece of him left untouched. One part of the wild boy that remained. And he was going to burn that part with iron, to brand it until only blackness remained, because of what happened to me.

My breath is trapped, held captive by the grief I feel for that small part.

I worried he didn't exist anymore, but he did. He's standing five feet away from me.

"Wait," I tell him. "Don't do this. You don't have to—"

"I do," he says softly, not turning to me again. That part is over.

Then he walks out the door, leaving me staring at the place where he stood.

The room is bathed in shadows, more dark than light. I step out of bed to the soft carpet, feeling it thick beneath my toes. I cross to the bathroom, blinking at the over-bright light. I face the wide mirror and lift my T-shirt by its hem.

I read what he's written backwards. A proof.

A simple proof, from the trigonometry book. I shouldn't even remember it. He definitely shouldn't. Unless he looked up the book later. Unless he read it again and again. But why would he do that?

The answer filters into my mind like sunlight through dust motes, caught and held before shining again. Of course the numbers haven't left me. There they are, as clear to me as the sun.

Damon must not have doubted that.

As I stare at the scrawled ink on my skin, my doubt fades away. It's replaced by the confidence that let me challenge Damon Scott to a poker game. The confidence that's let me survive the west side all these years.

And now Damon has gone to kill his own father. To become the monster he's fought his whole life. Will he ever stop saving me? If he becomes a murderer, he might. If he kills Jonathan Scott, he'll lose his last shred of humanity. I have to protect him the way he protected me.

Chapter Sixteen

Somehow I went for years without seeing Damon Scott.

He hovered low in my mind, the same quiet and insistent worry that I have knowing children in the city are hungry, knowing animals are in pain. He wasn't my waking thought, my nighttime prayer. He didn't take up every moment.

The next five days may as well be eternity. I stay locked up with Avery in Gabriel's home, which may as well be a castle for how heavily guarded it is. It's hard for me to eat, to sleep, because I know that Damon Scott is on the verge of something horrible.

Avery takes very good care of me, like he thought she would. She doesn't question my worry or my lack of appetite, thinking I'm still recovering from the trauma.

My body heals more every day.

There's something I want more than my strength, than my pale skin in its former smoothness. Only the guilty can understand this. I want redemption. There's an emotional debt more pressing than money.

It was one thing to give Damon up when I was a child, alone in the trailer.

Another when I'm almost a grown woman.

I need to get out of this place, but I can't do it alone, not with trained guards patrolling the perimeter. I watch them out the window when Avery thinks I'm mostly comatose, but that doesn't reveal any answers. They seem to vary up their schedules, as if they know someone might try to enter.

As if they know someone might try to escape.

Avery doesn't mean me any harm, that much I believe. But she's as much a prisoner here as I am. Neither of us can leave. She's the only one with any access to the outside world—a cell phone that she carries with her almost everywhere.

I know she texts her friend from college, because she tells me about some of them.

Other times her brow furrows, worry tinting her hazel eyes. She doesn't tell me what she texts when she gets like this. I don't know what she's afraid of, but it's something.

She looks up from her phone, her gaze beseeching.

"Come for a walk with me," she says.

It's something we've done before. Walks around the mansion. Through the garden. There's even a maze made out of hedges. I swear, the things rich people think of to get rid of their money. It's like they don't know what to do with it all.

But I don't know why she's whispering. Who does she think will hear her?

The line of her throat moves as she swallows. "I want to find out where the voices are coming from," she says, her voice shaky. "Will you help me?"

A shiver runs through me. What voices? I haven't said much. Only Damon seems to thaw me enough to speak, but I know this is important. Important because I can help her, maybe. The way she's been helping me.

Important because I can help Damon, who's out with Gabriel in the bowels of the city, searching through rundown tenements and alleys for a modern-day dragon.

Smart people don't always have perspective.

It had been a declaration. Does he love me? As a woman or as a child?

I'm not sure he knows, not sure it matters what name we put on it. It was the most unassuming gift he could have given me, one without any expectation that it would be returned. Thinking that I'm too young or maybe just too innocent to give it back.

Except I'm not the only smart person without perspective.

He knows I need him, but the truth is he needs me, too.

Avery leans close, something close to panic in her eyes. "You don't hear them, do you?"

I'm afraid she might come apart if I tell her the truth. The house is painfully silent. It hurts me, that's how silent it is. The lack of sound a physical presence, as if the world has become muted.

We're underwater here.

I'm desperate to find a way to her phone. The words to confide my plan on the tip of my tongue. I don't think she'll want to go along with me—her faith in Gabriel is too complete.

Aid comes from one of the least likely places. One of the guards appears in the doorframe. "Someone's at the gate," he says, making it clear he'd rather turn them away.

Some old friend of Avery's has come to visit her. More than a friend, if I read her hesitation right.

It would be an entertaining power play to watch—the guard who could probably bench press three hundred pounds and the young woman with her quiet control. And it's the perfect cover for me to slip her phone beneath the pillow. My hand moves maybe two inches. Neither of them notice.

"I'll stand outside the room," the guard says, deference winning. "With the door open."

Avery's voice is kind, gracious in her victory. "Thank you."

It takes forever for the guest to be searched for weapons. So long I'm afraid that Avery will look for her phone. I can't let her notice that it's under the pillow. She wouldn't suspect me of anything, mostly because she thinks I'm half brain dead. But it would ruin my chance.

I have to distract her. "Who is he?"

"An old boyfriend," she says, her cheeks turning pink.

"Oh." Gabriel won't be happy about that when he finds out.

Her eyes look lighter when she's curious. "Do you... do you have one? A boyfriend?"

I've been so deep underwater that I haven't even thought about him.

Guilt whispers through me. Brennan would

have worried about me. The first night, the second. It's been five days. Does he think I'm dead? Daddy must think so, when I left with Jonathan Scott and didn't come back. I don't feel as bad about that, since he's the reason I'm in this mess.

Encased in ice, I could spare myself that acidic mixture of worry and shame. Now it comes rushing back like bile, promising that every step on land would hurt. I could transform into a human again, but I would pay the price in pain. There's too much blood in the water to emerge unscathed.

When the security guard takes Avery away, I don't waste any time.

The number comes from memory. My fingers don't tremble as I dial the number. That's the only nod to confidence. Inside I'm a mess of fear and dread and worst of all hope.

"Hello?" The hoarse word tells a long story of the past five days.

"Daddy, it's me."

The pause that follows hangs heavy overhead. Storm clouds. North winds. "Is it—how are—oh God, Penny. I didn't know if you were—"

He can't seem to finish a sentence. The worst part is that I can't finish it for him, not with the knot in my throat. Not with the tangle in my mind, where familial love crosses accusation, a biological short-circuit.

"I'm alive," I manage to say.

"Where are you? Can you come home?"

Home. The word pings around inside me, unable to land anywhere. In the apartment with weak locks and cracks in every window? The lumpy armchair where Daddy sits each night? The Rubik's Cube. That had been home for a little girl desperate to find herself.

"Did you bring the money to Damon Scott?"

A terrible pause. "I looked for him, Penny. I swear I did. He went underground. Everyone said he couldn't be found when he didn't want to be."

"And then you spent it." There's no anger in my voice, not anymore.

Only resignation.

"No," he says, urgent and sincere. "I tried to find Jonathan Scott then, to give the money back to him. To tell him the deal was off. To *find* you. But he was gone, too."

Uncertainty wraps itself around me, warm and almost… comforting. Maybe ten thousand dollars doesn't matter in the large scheme of things, but it feels like I earned that money. It feels like it matters. "Where's the money now?"

"It's here. God, I've been so afraid that someone would know. That sounds crazy. It's not like I could ever hold onto a dollar longer than an hour. But I just... I've been sitting here, keeping it, thinking you were dead."

His voice breaks, but it doesn't sound like the end. It sounds like a continuation.

This is where we've always been. I can't walk away from the only family I have, from a person who actually cares about me. When Damon braced his body above me in his bed I had felt like a woman, grown and even sexual.

Now as I cling the phone I'm painfully aware that I'm fifteen, that my bed has pink sheets. That I'm only a girl who dreams about having her mama back.

That I want nothing more than a daddy who loves me.

Who am I to dream I could save Damon Scott?

Who am I to dream at all?

HE FINDS ME on the balcony, a wide marble-floored space with a carved stone balcony. From here I can see the expansive grounds—a lush garden and elaborate hedge maze. Rolling green hills and woods beyond. A view that carefully hides security cameras and armed patrols, an electric fence hidden in the tree line. Such deadly beauty.

I feel him before I see him, that prickling awareness that can only be Damon Scott. I'm sitting on an ornate metal chair, carving of Olympic gods cradling me with surprising comfort.

Footsteps come close and then stop. It must be my imagination that senses his heat. He's still a few feet away at least. How can he heat me up like no one else?

"Avery says you aren't eating," he says finally.

She worries about me, which is sweet. I don't really know what to do with that. I've had friends before, like Jessica. Even Brennan, but there's always a careful distance. Growing up in the west side, we all know not to get too close.

"I'm eating enough."

"She says there are nightmares."

"Aren't there?" I ask softly. "For you?"

That finally brings him around in front of me. It's a shock to see him in daylight, maybe for the first time. The sunlight makes his black hair gleam. His eyes look almost luminous out here, but calming, the contrast to the sun a relief.

"I've had nightmares," he says, his voice distant.

Unemotional, even though I know that's a lie. No one experiences what we have and comes out unscathed. Avery talked to me about seeing a counselor, asked if I wanted one, but I can't imagine what acceptance would look like.

Oh, that black pool with green tiles? Sure, I had a rough time almost drowning. I'm over it now. Anyone who says that is lying, so what's the point?

He looks cold and removed, like he has somehow achieved the impossible.

It makes me want to tear him down.

"Tell me," I demand.

For a moment I think he's going to refuse. He's going to keep that wall between us, thin now but crucial. Whatever we were before this— friends, potential lovers. Enemies. We've shared something now. We're both survivors.

Then he sits down, the softest sound of his breath releasing. And in that sound I hear the wall come down. I feel it, erased from existence—if only for this moment. It makes every nerve ending tingle along my arms, my stomach. He's been nearer to me than two feet away, but never as truly close as this.

"It started when I was five," he says, breaking my heart in that one emotionless statement. "I'm not sure what happened before then. Nothing good, I'm sure. But I remember the training that started at five."

"Training?" I say, horrified, terrified, but needing this. This connection.

"He said it would make me stronger. That people out in the world would hurt me. That I had to get strong enough to withstand them."

My stomach turns over. "I'm sorry."

"We practiced every day in that pool. There were other parts of the training. Other things I had to be ready for. In the other rooms, there's equipment that—"

"Please stop." I've heard enough for today. For a lifetime. *And you only have to listen. He had to live through it.* "How do you live with it?"

He looks at me then, his brow cocked in question. "What other choice is there?"

Dying, but I don't say that. It sounds too dramatic, and besides, I don't want to die. That's not what I'm really asking. I'm asking how to stop the nightmares. "I feel safe when you're with me."

Because he's the only one who understands.

No, that's not entirely true. Even before this happened I felt safe when he was around. Not safe with the way he made my body feel or what he let my father borrow. Safe in that I know no one can touch me when he's around—not even his father.

Damon is the only man on earth who would be *glad* to see Jonathan Scott. That would mean he could kill him. Or worse, probably. He might use some of that equipment.

"You shouldn't," he says, his voice hoarse. "I let you down."

"No, you got me out of there."

"Don't. Don't pretend like I did you any fucking favors. What you went through before I got there… That's been harder to live with than anything that came before."

It's more than feeling safe. I finally feel *warm* when he's around, my very own heat source. And it wasn't my body that came out of that pool. It was something reptilian. Cold blooded. I can't keep myself warm; I need him to do it for me.

"Stay with me," I ask, my voice breaking. "Like that first night. When you were with me, I didn't have the nightmares. You keep them away."

You keep him *away.*

"It's during nights that he comes out of hiding," Damon says, his voice tortured. "That's when I need to look for him. It's my only chance to find him."

"I need you more," I whisper.

He makes a low growling sound. "Don't fight me on this. I almost lost you."

"You're losing me now."

His jaw clenches, a muscle moving beneath three days' growth. "Once I'm done I'll stay with you. I'll protect you. But I need to do this first. I need to kill him."

He can't let it go. His anger has dug a hollow through him, as surely as little feet beneath the swing. "More than kill him, I'm guessing."

It's a merciless smile he gives me. "More than that."

This is his addiction. No needles or cards. Hating his father. Hunting him.

And he was choosing it over me.

"No," I say, almost desperate. "If you do this you'll become him. That's what he wants. That's what he's always wanted."

"Maybe I could have escaped it," Damon says, almost melancholy. "Except he touched you. And there's no way I can let that stand. No way I can let him live."

Which is exactly why Jonathan Scott had taken me.

Somehow, he had known that.

Damon stands, almost pushing back against the sunlight, as if the rays hurt him. And I realize with horror that they might. How much sunlight did he get as a child? "I hope one day I'm the man you deserve."

"And until then?" I ask, the knot in my throat so thick and so rough.

"Until then I'll make this right the only way I know how."

Chapter Seventeen

GABRIEL MILLER'S HOUSE is a sprawling modern mansion, designed with so many twists and turns they must be intentional. He wants people to be lost, to be intimidated, and it works.

I have a path of breadcrumbs using the abstract art decorating the cherry wood walls—splashes of red against swaths of black. Pops of yellow. I can make it to the kitchen on my own, not that I go there often.

And I can find Avery's room when I need her, although I never do at night.

Gabriel keeps her well occupied in the evenings when he returns from searching for Jonathan Scott. Whether I have nightmares or restless insomnia, I don't follow the hushed words and the moans down the hallway.

Those times are the hardest, when I feel so alone my chest aches.

This is what I always feared. Mama leaving me. Daddy, too. He chose his addiction over my safety. I can't decide whether that makes him weak or just human.

My only solace comes from a stack of books on the side table.

The only books remotely mathematical in nature are about stock charts and economics. They're even more dry and obtuse than the automotive books, but I revel in them like they're sun after a long rain.

There are a few books I remember were on the syllabus in English class this year. *Grapes of Wrath* doesn't hold my interest, but I keep it there anyway. It serves the same purpose as my self-enforced bedtime in that trailer—pretending like there's a grownup to guide me.

I wander down to the library after lunch, carrying the stack of books.

A fire crackles beneath the large marble mantel. Someone must be here. I take a step backward, prepared to leave. Avery peers around the wide leather wing of an armchair. "Hey, you. Don't go."

Hesitant, I hover beneath the arched doorway.

Avery's been incredibly kind to me, even nurturing, but it only makes me conflicted. I wanted that kind of nurturing from Mama. And occasionally I'd even get it, when she was between boyfriends. But I learned not to trust in it. It would be snatched away when I needed it most.

"What do you have there?" she asks, looking at my books with interest.

The urge to share with her is too strong, to show her what I like and find out what she does. I approach the rug with slow steps, feeling almost shy.

The library is massive, two stories connected by a carved spiral staircase. And on the second floor, the shelves go so high you have to use a ladder to reach the very top. Small leather benches set off the different bookcases, which is where I would usually sit.

In the center of the room is a plush rug that holds two oversized armchairs and a circular table. An intricate carved chess set sits there, positioned so the people in the chairs can play.

Avery points to the empty chair beside her. "Join me. Please."

In a rush I settle into the cushion, sinking deep. "I'm sorry. I don't want to disturb you."

"You're not." She tilts her head, reading the spines of the books I'm holding. "You found Gabriel's financial books."

"Do you think he'd mind?" I ask, holding the books tighter.

She laughs. "I'm sure he wouldn't. In fact he'd probably love to discuss them with you. He's kind of a numbers junkie, but it's all over my head."

There's a book in her lap, with plain text on the front.

"Athenian Vase Painting," I say, reading the cover aloud.

"It's my guilty pleasure," she says, not sounding very guilty. "The classical section of the library is incredible, if you're interested in the subjects. I can point out some of the more accessible books. This one's a little dense."

"Does Gabriel like ancient history?"

"No, but he likes making me happy," she says with a private smile. "It used to be my major in college. Before I—well, before I left."

"Why did you stop?"

She sucks in a breath as I realize my mistake. I've cared too much, revealed too much. And worst of all, I've reminded her of something dark.

"I'm sorry," I add quickly, starting to stand. "Never mind."

"No, please. It's not your fault." Her hazel eyes look so sad I have to sit again. And I recognize something in her words, that longing. Loneliness. "I had to leave when my dad lost his court case. And he was hospitalized. Long story short I used my college fund to help us keep the house as long as we could."

I look away, remembering that story in the local news. Everyone had been talking about it. The famous businessman and politician, known for his works of charity, convicted of embezzlement. And despite that he had escaped jail time. The benefits of being rich.

"You've heard the rest of the story," she says, reading my expression.

"Not really," I say quickly. "People talk, but I don't believe them."

"In this case they were probably telling the truth. I approached Damon Scott about a loan. Which he wouldn't give me since I had no way to pay it back. Gabriel was there. He suggested that I auction my virginity."

A memory uncoils inside me, stealing my breath.

You know he doesn't have a way to pay you back. How dare you loan him money?

Would you have preferred I told him no? He would have gone straight to my father, who would have charged him higher interest than I did.

I had been so furious then, so sure of my rightness. And now? I didn't know the answer. There was no solution to my father's addiction.

There was no proof against heartache.

"So that's how I ended up here," she says, gesturing to the library, the mansion itself.

I've seen her and Gabriel together, the way he looks at her, as if she owns him. He isn't forcing her to do anything. At least, not anymore. "Do you ever think you'll leave?"

Her expression turns faraway. "I'm not sure. I mean, don't get me wrong. I'm happy here. It's beautiful and luxurious and safe. But sometimes I miss school so much it hurts." She glances down at the book in her lap. "Books aren't the same. They're nice, though."

I reach across the chess board and take her hand.

She looks up at me, her eyes wide with surprise. It might be the first time I've touched her. The first time I've touched anyone, since the attack.

Footsteps startle me, and I turn to see Gabriel stride into the library. He makes a straight line toward Avery, a living and breathing shortest-path algorithm.

He bends down, one hand behind her neck to keep her close. A kiss on her cheek. A whisper in her ear that makes her blush. Only then does he straighten and give me a kind, "Hello, Penny."

I'm a little disappointed Damon isn't with him. Maybe a lot disappointed. "Hi."

"What are you two doing?" he asks.

"Talking about Damon," Avery says, before I can respond. "And how he auctioned me off."

It shouldn't surprise me that she's keeping secrets—even if those secrets are only what's in her heart. She doesn't want him to know that she longs for school. Because he would be angry? Or because she would feel disloyal?

I'm hardly one to judge. I don't share what's in my heart very much. I barely know what's there, most of the time. For me that's the top-most shelf, full of dust, requiring the use of a special ladder just to reach it.

Gabriel gives a small smile, completely unrepentant. "He gave me a lot of grief for that."

"Did he?" I ask, uncertain why Damon would mind. It made sense that he wouldn't want to give Avery money if he knew she would never be able to repay. But how could he mind the auction? I have no doubt that he profited from it.

"He can be a little protective of women. He's been that way for as long as I've known him." Something about Gabriel's golden eyes invites me in, as if he's imparting an important secret.

"But he owns a strip club."

"More than one," Gabriel says with a nod. "And for a girl in a desperate situation, there's no place safer or more lucrative for her to be. You should have seen how selective he was about the guest list for the auction."

"Really?" Avery says, sounding surprised.

Dark flecks of gold glint in Gabriel's eyes. "I don't think he knew whether to be relieved or worried when I won. He warned me that if I hurt you, I'd have to answer to him."

"Well," Avery says, her voice arch. "Then there are a few things I'll have to tell him about."

The smile flirting with her lips says she's only teasing. Though I suspect if I were to dig, Gabriel has done one or two things that hurt her. He clenches a fist in her hair, pulling her back to whisper something else in her ear. She's scarlet by the time he led her upstairs, giving me a short, "We'll see you tomorrow. Mrs. B is in the kitchen if you need anything."

"Go to bed early," Avery says, her voice trailing into the room as she's led away. "I know you're feeling better, but your body is still recovering."

I put my hand over my mouth to hide my smile, but it's there, blinding and unstoppable. They're so sweet together. Almost enough to break through the ice around me, even without Damon Scott around. *Almost.*

I READ A well-worn copy of *Quantitative Risk Analysis* late into the night, past dog-ears and highlighted lines. Gabriel knows this book well. Only a few times do I stop and leave notes in the margins, adding to what his sprawling script has written.

Once I correct him, laying out my argument in a few lines, wondering if he'll ever find this. They're a different kind of breadcrumb. My kind.

By the time I get to the chapter on volatility in valuation, it's midnight.

My eyelids slip lower and lower with every slow blink. I can't think anymore tonight.

Can't use the numbers to keep away the loneliness.

I reach over and flip off the lamp, dousing the room in shadows. I keep the bathroom light on all night, a holdover from the first days after the attack. From longer than that, if I'm honest. The light that slid between my plastic blinds was a comfort. And the heavy drapes in this house, the tinting on the rooms, the luxury of darkness that rich people seem to crave sometimes feels like a muzzle.

Sleep laps its gentle waves against me. There are no strong currents on the surface. It's deceptive, how softly it lulls me. How many times will I believe and hope and pray to find peace there? To drift on the lazy river of my mind.

No matter how softly it begins I'm always dragged under.

The dream comes in a tidal wave, wrapping my body in terror.

In my dream I'm back in the mental hospital. In my dream, I never left. The walls are coated with something black and pungent, the floor slick. Pain slices my scalp as he drags me by my hair.

He strides with cool familiarity through the hallways, like he's been here a million times. Like he *lives* here. My body may as well be on fire, that's how much the pain and fear scorch me, that's how much I scream. In the molten center is the certainty that Damon Scott went through this.

Not something similar. This exactly. In this horrible place.

He knows these walls. These floors.

He knows the cracked placard that says *Recreation Room* in front of us.

There are a million funhouse horrors that a recreation room might hold. They flash through my brain like a demented slideshow, promising that this will be worse than what came before— worse than the stabbing pain in my body and the shame in my heart. And even so, I could not have predicted this.

I could not have foretold about the pool.

It's large and rectangular, like the kind at my YMCA. Only instead of pale white concrete it's made from tile, green and thin and cracked in a thousand places. Nothing that could be operational today. And it's not operational, strictly speaking. There isn't water. There couldn't be water, not with the thick cracks in the concrete. As if the whole foundation has shifted over the decades, nature reclaiming what was hers.

I want to slide into the cracks, even though they're a couple inches wide. I want to disappear into the center of the earth. He told me I'd want to die, and he's right, he's right, he's right.

He tosses me into the pit. My knees make a loud *crack* with the fall. I know there's pain, but it doesn't register. Not with anticipation clawing at my throat, knowing what will come next. The pool may be empty, but there's something a little damp down here. A little slippery. I stagger, trying to stand, struggling to find that sliver of hope that says I'll make it out alive.

"Don't worry," he says, soft enough I almost don't hear. "This will help you, too."

In the corner the thick roots of a tree have broken through the tile in the far end, leaving a wide chasm. That split narrows to a thick crack near the bottom. A little more and water wouldn't hold.

The monster above me turns a knob.

A steel pipe juts out of the wall. It pours water into the pool, leaving a small puddle at my feet. My heart beats a slow rhythm, like it can't believe this. Like it knows better than to panic.

Like this can't possibly be real.

When I was little I fought the current. I kicked and paddled, struggling to get to the surface. Now I stand very still as the water rises to my ankles, knowing it won't possibly help.

There aren't sharp rocks at the bottom. Only a dark vegetation grown over tile.

Water rises, dark in the ancient *Recreation Room*, almost as black as the bottom. The mermaid tank was beautiful, mostly because the water was clear. And I knew the river was different because it was dark. Like this.

And then Jonathan Scott reaches for a lever. There's something metal and thin leaning against the wall above me. My mind can't process what it is. My mind doesn't *want* to process what it is, even as he lowers the grate over the top of the pool.

Some dark part of me recognizes it as some primitive safety device.

That dark part of me laughs.

The water level will rise. The grate will keep me under water. "Please no," I whisper, unable to stop myself. There's no way it will work, no way I can stop myself from trying.

He looks almost sad. "Don't panic. You'll only lose your head."

My nails press so hard into my palms they draw blood. There will be crescent shaped wounds in my hands, but I won't be alive to see them. "Don't do this to me," I say, my voice shaking. "I'll do anything. Anything."

"You'll do everything, lovely peach."

What does he want from me? *What does he want from Damon?* The water tickles my knees, weirdly harmless as it rises. Deadly once it's done. "I'll make the money back. Work in the clubs. For sex. Anything. Don't do this to me. *Please.*"

"Do you know, when I first got here, they still did lobotomies. How barbaric is that?"

"*This* is barbaric," I scream at him. "Let me out. Oh my God, let me out of here."

Lobotomies. Is that what happened to him? Is that why he's insane?

He smiles a little, like he can read my thoughts. "They did many cruel things, but not this. This was beautiful. I fought it at first. That's the weakness inside us. It's a gift to make you stronger."

This is how Damon learned to hold his breath so long. This is what he ran away from. This very pool with its green tile and black water. *And this is why I deserve what's happening.* Because I sent him here. He came back to this for me.

Chapter Eighteen

"**T**RIGONOMETRY," SAYS A voice in the darkness.

For one bittersweet moment I flash into the past, a little girl lost, afraid and alone. With only a wild boy to save me. He had seemed like not enough at first. And then he'd been all I wanted.

I sit up in bed, my gaze finding a silhouette in the corner.

There's no wild boy left in him. Even in shadow he's made of long planes and crisp corners. He reclines in a chair, his long leg kicked out, one hand dangling down holding a glass. His other hand holds a book open, a stark sliver of light across the white page.

You came back, I want to shout.

Except that might make him leave. Maybe he actually is still wild underneath all that expensive linen and wool. I have to tread carefully so I don't spook him.

And so that I don't make him pounce.

"That's what you were doing at six years old. I

guess it's no surprise you're doing—" He pauses, glancing back at the hard cover. "Financial Engineering. What the fuck is that?"

"I thought you were in business with Gabriel," I say, surprised my voice is so even.

To find him in my room like this is a dream. I'm not sure whether it's a good dream or a bad one, but I never expected it to happen. Not once. Definitely not twice in my life.

He gives a low laugh. "He's the one who handles the investments. My side of the business is a little more… well, let's just say hands-on."

"Avery told me about your strip clubs." I infuse the words with all the disdain I feel. And hide all of the horribly misplaced jealousy. There's no reason to mind that he's seen naked women.

No point in thinking a girl like me would ever have claim on a man like this.

"It's mostly addition in strip clubs," he says, sounding playful. "Very large numbers, though. I'm sure you can imagine."

"I'm sure I *can't* imagine." Not only because it requires being naked in front of strange men. Because we've never had large numbers of money.

It's only been small numbers. Only subtraction.

"Simple math," he continues. "No trigonometry required. No calculus."

"Calculus *is* simple," I can't resist saying, even though I know it's a red flag.

And he's the bull, charging forward with a charming smile and sharp teeth. "Just because you can do something doesn't mean it's easy, baby genius."

Something ignites inside me when he says that. It makes me argue against him, if only so he'll argue back. "Calculus is just about continuity. About a line going on and on, never stopping. Never breaking."

There was a beauty to that flow, to the infinite approach.

He runs a thick square-tipped finger down the page, as if soaking up the information. And maybe he is. Because when he speaks he seems to know what it says. "Except it isn't real, is it? It's an ideal. A pipe dream. A perfect vision of the world that pretends jagged edges and broken pieces don't exist."

"Maybe some of us need that perfect vision." I can't pretend we're still talking about math.

"And maybe some of us know too much to be that naïve," he says softly.

I think I hate him in that moment. "You think I don't know about broken things? After what your father did? After he *broke* me?"

"You're not broken," Damon says sharply.

A startled laugh bursts from me. "I'm not the only one naïve, if you believe that."

"You are," he says, sounding fierce. "Still innocent. Still a baby."

"I'm *not* a baby."

There's something brewing inside me. Maybe anger. Definitely excitement. I can't really place the feeling, except that every time he calls me a baby I want to hit him. But I also want him to keep doing it.

He sounds almost regretful. "Fifteen years old. That's a baby."

There's a wall between us, built out of fear and doubt and an age difference that will never really go away. I'm getting older, but so is he. That wall should have been enough to keep me from being interested. Instead it feels like I've been leaning against that wall for years.

And sometimes it feels like he's right on the other side.

"Today's my birthday," I say, swallowing after the words are out.

It feels like a risk, sharing something like that. Even though it's ordinary information. This time last year I had been at the burger place with

Brennan. We started *dating* in middle school, even though it mostly consisted of holding hands in the hallways.

This year I'm in a modern-day castle, half guest of honor, half prisoner.

He snaps the book shut. "What?"

"My birthday," I say, trying to sound old and unaffected like it doesn't mean anything.

A curse word hovers in the darkness. "Did you have cake? Candles? Presents?"

A shrug. "I didn't have those things at home. Why would I have them here?"

"Avery would have done something—"

"I didn't tell her."

"Why not?"

Because I didn't want her to worry about me. And because I'm the one worried about her. She's clearly going through something, but she's hiding it from Gabriel. The only reason I know is because I'm mostly silent in her company. Mostly watching. "Does it matter?"

"You turned sixteen."

I can't help the pleased smile that crosses my face. He shouldn't see something as vulnerable as that, but it comes out anyway. I am pleased to be sixteen. Despite what's happened to me, despite what Daddy's done. It's a bright spot, being older.

It feels like maybe I'm a woman.

Except when Damon stands up and crosses the room. Then I feel small and unsure again.

"You deserve a celebration," he says, his voice biting. "A party with your friends."

"What friends?" I say, unable to name a single person other than the one in this room.

"You have friends. From school. From the diner. And you have that boyfriend. What's his name? Bennet?"

The air seems thick, making my chest rise and fall with each breath. "Brennan."

"That's right. Would he have given you a birthday kiss?"

And just like that the suggestion blooms between us, that Damon could kiss me. That he could do it right now. We're only three feet away. So little space between us. So impossible to cross.

"Yes," I say, more breath than sound.

Brennan would have kissed me on my birthday. It would have made me feel safe. I know without trying that Damon's kiss wouldn't make me feel that way.

Damon sits on the edge of the bed, in the same way Daddy did. When I would have a screaming nightmare after Mama left. When he would comfort me.

There's nothing comforting about this.

And Damon, though they inhabit the same dark world, he's nothing like Daddy. He has complete control over himself, over the people around him. In fact the only person he can't control is Jonathan Scott. Maybe that's why it's his obsession to hunt him down.

He uses that control now, a subtle direction as he leans forward.

And I find myself canting forward.

He would never be as crass as to give orders. Never be as rough as to drag me by my hair. But it's an order all the same, one my body responds to as surely as physical force.

"You're really young," he remarks, sounding casual.

Only his eyes show the truth of him, the lust and frustration that swirl in the black depths. There's something else, too. A kind of desolation that can only be seen when he's inches away.

How many other people get this close to him? Not many, I'm guessing.

It's no coincidence he prefers his women dancing onstage, him in the shadows.

"If I'm so young, why are you here?" I ask, unable to tear my gaze away, hardly able to blink.

He laughs. "I don't fucking know."

And maybe he was right, before, when he called me a baby. That's what I had been, with Brennan. Using him as a security blanket. Even when I thought I might have sex with Damon, when I imagined it, it was some theoretical construct. The curve on a graph, its every point carefully plotted and explained.

Real life could never be that pure. Who would want that?

For the first time, my body becomes aware of him as a man. Of myself as a woman. Birthdays have never felt like big occasions for me. Mathematically one day out of three hundred and sixty-five isn't significant. Except I've never felt like this before. Whether it's because I turned sixteen today or because Damon is looking at me with pure hunger, I feel ready for him.

"I know why," I whisper.

"Of course you do." The words are condescending, but the way he says them isn't. There's a quiet confidence in him, almost pride, as if he likes me being smart. As if it affects him the same away his crisp suits and beautiful smile affect me.

Everything about him in his moment invites my secrets.

Like this one: "I dream about you."

His breath catches. "Don't tell me that. What

I'll do to you—"

"Do you dream about me?"

"Never," he says, his voice harsh.

In the heartbeat that follows my world crumbles. I'm standing in the rubble when he runs a hand through his hair. When he says, "I could never let myself. Not if I wanted to leave you alone."

My hand reaches out, before I've really planned it. Before I've really thought through what it means. To touch him. To *feel* him, his heat and his heart. Two fingers pressing against the perfectly smooth fabric of his shirt. He's so solid beneath those white dress clothes. As strong and as wide as I would have dreamed my wild boy would be, grown into a man.

"I'm afraid to be alone."

His eyes burn. "You will *never* be alone. I swear that to you. I would never let that happen. But you deserve to have a normal life. That's what I want for you."

"Does what I want matter?"

He laughs. "You don't know what you're asking for."

I don't know where the boldness comes from, but there's too much of it. I'm overflowing with the desire to ask for what I want, to demand what

I need. Is this what sixteen feels like? "A kiss."

A rough sound. "What?"

"I'm asking for a kiss."

"Christ," he mutters. "You're so innocent."

Challenge simmers around us, sparkling and hot. "Then do it. What will it hurt?"

"It will hurt," he says, capturing my face with careful movements, his hand cupping my whole jaw. He tilts me only the slightest angle, but it changes everything. Thirty degrees to the right. That's all it takes for me to open for his kiss. Made ready for him, my whole body brimming with anticipation.

He leans close, his gaze a dark promise.

One millimeter away from me, so close it hurts to be apart. Like our lips are magnets, trembling with an unseen force. His hand holds me away, that small amount. "Say no," he murmurs. "Scream. Fight me. Cry for me to stop."

"Is that how you like it?" I whisper, the words brushing my lips against his.

Only the smallest shake of his head. "I like you moaning and needy and begging me for more."

I can't imagine moaning. "How do you know?"

"Because I did dream of you, Penny. I dreamed of you and I watched you and I wanted you. Even though I knew it was wrong, I couldn't stop. It isn't about how old you are—it's you. It's only ever been you."

That's the last thing I hear before his lips press against mine. Then there's only empty sky in my head, only starlight, only a vast and pulsing space. There are no walls here. Nothing that could possibly separate us. His mouth so hot against mine that I'm melting, turned liquid in his hard grip.

Square inch by square inch, my body relaxes. Only then do I realize how tense I was. How tense I've been my whole life, braced for something awful to happen.

As if he were waiting for that sign, Damon moves against me. A new configuration of his mouth against mine, a new kind of kiss, every curve completely distinct. Pleasure sparks across my lower lip, and I realize he tasted me. *Oh God, his tongue. He touched me with his tongue.*

My lips part on a gasp, whether from sensation or shock.

He takes the advantage, nudging my mouth open. Opening me like a petal grown wide and blooming. Then his tongue touches mine. My whole body changes then, becomes something flushed and alive, every cell breathing for the first time. There are feelings in new places, a heat between my legs, a terrible tension that I think only he can fix for me.

I've touched myself under the covers before, but it's never *hurt* like this.

There's something happening inside. A change.

A sound breaks through the silence, low and sensual. *It's me.*

And just like that he sits back. In the space he had been there's only empty space. My breathing comes fast, my whole body aching and hot. I feel like he took me apart and put me back together. A child before. A woman now. And every womanly part of me attuned to him, wanting more.

He breathes hard, staring at me with something like desperation. "Fuck," he says.

"Please more," I say, before I even know that I'm pleasing him. Before I see the flash of pure desire in his dark eyes. *I like you moaning and needy and begging me for more.*

How much more could he make me do?

He stands, abrupt and impersonal. "That's enough."

"That's enough," I repeat, my voice hollow.

"That's what you have to say to me?"

A cruel smile mars his beautiful face, and even before he speaks, I know it will cut me. "What do you want to hear? That kissing you was so magical that I never want to touch another woman, never want to look at one? That you're the only person I've ever wanted this badly?"

I flinch at his tone, but it's a mistake. It's blood in the water. "Don't be like that."

"Oh, but that's what I am. Remember? I'm a criminal. A cold-blooded killer. So callous that I took money from a sad old man who can't fucking stop gambling the money that should feed his daughter."

The reminder of my daddy makes my breath catch. There's something that can pierce the haze of desire. Grief can do it. A grief so hard and tight it's a fist in my chest. "You didn't take it. You gave him money."

"You're right," he says, his voice silky smooth. So like his father it slices me open. Like two hands on either side of a wound, pulling the skin apart. "I gave him money he could never repay. Because there's something I want more than his debt. There's you."

I'm completely flat. Two dimensional. Made into an object without value.

"Stop it," I whisper.

"That's not what you were saying a few minutes ago."

"And this isn't what *you* were saying a few minutes ago," I say, tears hot against my eyelids.

"True. There's something painfully sweet about your little jailbait mouth. But I can't let you distract me. Not with Jonathan Scott still roaming the streets."

That's what this is about. His father. *His hunt.*

And that look in his eyes—I recognize it too well. The one Mama would get before she found a new boyfriend with new needles. The one Daddy gets before the rent money disappears. There's always an addiction. And God, the books on the nightstand prove no one's really immune.

"Then stay," I say, more afraid for him than myself. There's a reckless aura around him. A violence that seems almost directed at himself—or the man who made him that way. "Stay here with me."

He gives me a crooked smile, eerie because of how sweet it looks. "No, baby genius. You know the answer is no. I have something else to do first."

"You're not a killer. You said you were, but you're not."

I don't know if I'm trying to convince him or me. How could I love a murderer?

"I'm not?" he says, almost idly. What he shows me next takes my breath away. It's hard to hold his gaze, to stare into the terrible soul he shows me. "I've never killed before now. But I think I'm going to enjoy this. I'll draw it out, make it last. And when I come back this will finally be over."

He leaves the room with that threat in the air.

With that imagery in my mind. *Torture.* The kind of torture that Jonathan Scott did to me. The kind he must have done to his own son for years. It's a form of justice, a balance to the equation. But it will turn Damon into the same monster he's hunting. It will break this man as surely as his father broke me.

CHAPTER NINETEEN

I SPEND THE next few days in a kind of stunned purgatory. My mind replays that kiss over and over again, recalling the silver flecks in his eyes I could only see that close, the slightly mint flavor of his breath. A thousand details my mind catalogued for me to look through, hour after hour, minute after minute.

And every daydream ends the same way.

With the nightmare of me in that black pool, fighting to breathe.

Avery has downloaded these books on her phone about PTSD and repressed memories. She reads them out loud to me, but I'm not really sure if they're for me or her.

It takes days before her worry level starts to rise.

Breaking out of this gilded cage will require more than ordinary worry.

Over a breakfast of oatmeal and grapefruit slices I say, "He's not coming back."

Her hazel eyes meet mine, panic pure and

strangely beautiful. "Penny?"

I pick up my spoon, wondering about the best way to convince her. *Damon is going to crush the last small piece of his humanity torturing his father, who also happens to be after you.* No, she wouldn't rush to Jonathan Scott's aid. And that's the way she would see it.

He's not the one in danger. What he did to me, the way he violated me, it's unbearably intimate. He knows things about me, private things, but I know things too. Like the fact that he *wants* to die.

He wants to be tortured, for whatever insane reason is in his head.

"Why did you say that?" Avery demands. "What do you know?"

"He never said goodbye."

She gives me a hard look. "If you mean Gabriel, he's coming back. Any minute now."

"Him too."

"Penny. Who didn't say goodbye?"

"Damon."

She hides her relief. "Do you want him to come back?"

Only with every cell in my body.

I want him to come back whole, not as the monster he hunts. I shrug, swishing my oatmeal around in the bowl. Avery is always pushing me to eat more. Doesn't she realize that I've survived on less my whole life? This is what I need her help with—getting us out of this fortress so that we can find Damon.

"Maybe we can visit the Den one of these days. We'll get Gabriel to take us."

Does she really think that's how it will happen? That Damon will let us visit him for tea in the afternoon? That her precious Gabriel will come out of this unscathed? No, she *wants* to believe that. I understand about that. "He needs help."

She bites her lip. "Do you ever hear voices? Voices that aren't there?"

All the time, but not the way she means. I think she has repressed memories, ones that are coming out to haunt her. My memories live on the surface. They keep me cold company, even when I'm alone. "*You definitely can't trust me.*"

Her eyes widen. "What?"

I feel a little guilty for this, but I need Avery to be afraid.

Need her to understand the enemy the men are facing. It's not that he doesn't care about their souls. It's his goal to burn them. I understand Jonathan Scott in a way no one else does, maybe even his son.

"*Run and tell your daddy that Jonathan Scott is here.*"

Sometimes I wish I could push the memories down, the way she does. But that would be such a complete aloneness. I guess they bring me some comfort after all, memories of the terrible Jonathan Scott. I think I'm finally getting through to her when we hear footsteps outside.

I watch with an aching chest the hope across her face.

The doctor comes into the kitchen. *Hopes dashed.*

He looks as rough and jagged-edged as ever, his shirt sleeves rolled up revealing thick forearms and some kind of pale tattoo on his smooth freckled skin.

"How are you feeling?" he asks me.

I like Anders, because I don't have to pretend around him. Whatever's in my head, he seems to understand. "I used to dream about trees," I tell him, but I don't mean trees. I mean the wild boy who lived in them. The pretend-life we could have lived if he stayed. "About sunshine. And dirt."

He simply nods. "Better, then."

I am doing better, strangely better than Avery

herself. It seems strange, like maybe I should be more broken by what happened. Then again there's no timetable for recovery. "I know it doesn't sound pretty—dirt. The smell of it, thick and strong. It means you're free."

Even in my fantasies we don't live in a castle. If he had stayed we would have lived in the woods, would have fished in the lake, would have walked barefoot and wild.

THE GOOD NEWS is that Avery comes up with an elaborate plan to escape the mansion. That it's such a secret confirms every fear I've had about our positions here. Prisoners.

The bad news is that she thinks she's leaving without me.

I sneak after her and the security guard on her tail, making it into the trunk of the black SUV before the door closes.

"What are you doing?" Avery whispers, her eyes wide with surprise.

With a sigh I burrow myself into her body. She knows exactly what I'm doing.

After a moment her body relaxes, accepting me.

It's actually pretty impressive, the feint she set

up so they would think she left with a delivery truck from earlier. The security guard drives us off the property himself.

Less impressive when we sneak onto the streets of west side. That's where her plan ends, with two young women stranded in the worst part of town with no money. Only a rich girl, honestly.

"Tanglewood Sober Ride," I tell a surly bus driver, dragging Avery back with me before anyone can protest. The program is rarely used by people who actually should use it. More by people who want to joy ride on moldy old buses, which tells you everything you need to know about the state of the seats.

The bus shakes violently as it begins moving, knocking Avery off balance.

I drag her into the seat next to me.

"Thank you," she says, sounding breathless.

All I have for her is a small smile. We make a pretty good team, though I'm not going to tell her that. I hope we never have to break out of a multi-million-dollar home again.

"We should go to the Den," she says. "It's on Fourth Street, once you go past the train tracks and—"

I squeeze her hand. These are my stomping

grounds. "I know."

The buildings get more narrow as we approach the historic district. The alleyways more winding, every building with three secret exits leftover from the prohibition.

On Fourth Street I pull the cord, making the bus stop.

We reach the Den to find the door open, the fortress completely dark. Empty. At least that's how it looks from a few feet away. When we reach the short steps, we see him. Anders. The doctor. Spread out on the stairs like some kind of gruesome warning sign.

Avery kneels beside him, pressing her hands to his chest, coating her hands in blood. She takes off her sweater and pushes it against the wound.

He coughs. "Don't."

I can't help but think pain is a good sign at a time like this. It means he's alive and feeling. Then again that sounds like something Jonathan Scott would say.

"You're losing blood," Avery says, clearly panicking.

"Don't," he coughs again, his words mangled.

Panic descends on me like a heavy fog, keeping my feet in the same place, blurring my vision. It feels too much like being underwater, this fear.

Too heavy to possibly fight.

Avery looks back at me, as if I might have the answers.

"He's not here," I say, because I know he won't be upstairs.

"Gabriel?" she asks.

I shake my head. It's Damon. *It's always been Damon.*

Anders drags her close. "Don't go to him. That's what he wants."

That is what Jonathan Scott wants, but then he orchestrated this violence. He's the conductor, keeping all of us playing. We're all just instruments to him. Even Gabriel, rare and beautiful.

Avery calls the police while I consider bolting. I want to find Damon, to protect him. At the same time I want to run far away from here, to hide in the trees somewhere, to live off the ruined land.

The truth is that I will go find Damon. It was always leading to this.

I only don't want to take Avery with me. It's too dangerous. And she's too innocent.

Before I can make a decision, she turns to me. "He sent you to me, didn't he?"

There are pieces of her story available to me— the virginity auction that Damon Scott ran that sold her to Gabriel Miller. Her enmity with him, her eventual trust.

And now her capture in his castle.

"I don't know," I whisper, not entirely sure what connection she has to Jonathan Scott.

Her gaze is fierce. "You're going to take me to him."

"No," I say, shaking my head. She doesn't belong in that mental hospital.

In the end I know she'll come with me, the same way I came with her. We're two sides to the same coin. We both love dangerous men. We both will lose ourselves trying to save them.

✧   ✧   ✧

I STOP BY the diner to pick up a knife—a small weapon compared to the ones the men will have, but better than nothing. I also take the opportunity to talk to Jessica, who looks shocked to see me alive.

"What the hell did Damon do to you?" she demands.

I glance down to find blood on my hands, leftover from helping Anders get to a bed so he wouldn't bleed out. "It's not mine."

Her eyebrows shoot up. "Then what did you do to him?"

All I can do is laugh, which I know makes me look crazy. "I need to ask you something. How do you know if you love someone?"

She laughs too, a little disbelieving, mostly relieved. "Jesus, you gave me a heart attack. The only person I've ever loved is Ky. And that's… you know it's not a feeling. Not for me. It's just a state of being. Of turning to him, every second. Of wanting the best for him. Of wanting to give up everything for him."

Impulsively I give her a kiss on the cheek. "Thank you."

"Wait," she says, already sensing my exit. "What are you doing with a knife?"

We don't need to get into details, so I give her a small wave and return to the street. Avery waits for me, looking crazy nervous—which is a legit feeling, honestly. I know she's older than me, but I have this strange protective feeling. It's not the love that Jessica described, but it's something like that.

"When we get there," I tell her, "I'll go in first. I know the layout, at least a little bit. And there's always a chance it's rigged to explode or something crazy like that."

Her mouth drops open. "So you're going to sacrifice yourself?"

"It only makes sense."

"Are you kidding me? It makes zero sense. If anyone's going first, it's me."

"I'm nobody," I say softly, embarrassed I need to explain this. "The way that royalty would have someone taste their food, to make sure it wasn't poisoned."

Avery James wasn't born in the west side. She doesn't belong here. Her father was some famous businessman and politician, and even if he eventually lost everything, that doesn't change her pedigree.

"I'm not royalty," she says, sounding horrified. "And no one's going to die for me."

Maybe it's only girls like me who can see the class system, ones who know they'll never rise above it. "Maybe not royalty in the official sense. But in every way that counts. Girls like me, no one saves us in time."

"Damon did," she says, certain in this.

"He kept me from dying, but that's not what I needed saving from. What Jonathan did to me…" It wasn't about my body. It was my mind that he wanted. My mind he broke. Some twisted impulse to repeat what happens in that mental hospital. To make everyone else like him.

"God, Penny."

"So you see what I'm saying. I'm already damaged."

"Sometimes it's harder to survive," she says.

She does understand. For the first time I don't feel alone. "Yes."

"I won't let you martyr yourself for me. We go together, okay?"

After a long pause I take her hand. Together. That's how we'll do this. Some small part of my soul eases at the knowledge. And I realize that even with Daddy, with Mama, I have always been alone. Only now with these people, this group of criminals and fallen heiresses, do I feel like I could have a true family. The possibility hangs in the air as thick as the mist hovering over the streets.

Chapter Twenty

THE SMELL OF pain fills the air. Jonathan Scott is strung up by his wrists, shirtless and clearly beaten. His skin singed and turned black. How long have they been torturing him? By the dead look in Damon's eyes, it's been an eternity.

"What are you doing here?" Gabriel says when he sees us.

"Looking for you," Avery whispers, clearly in shock. "How long have you been here?"

"You shouldn't be here."

She takes a step forward "Is this…a hospital?"

Jonathan Scott begins to laugh, a horrifying sound. Blood-tinged spittle flies onto the floor. "Does someone look sick to you, little girl?"

"You're not looking very well at the moment," she says.

"I've never been well, not really. Neither have you."

Gabriel takes a step forward. "Don't speak to her. You don't fucking speak to her."

"Gabriel," she whispers. "What happened to

him? Look at all the open wounds, the burns, the blood. Did you do all of this?"

Heavy scars mangle Jonathan Scott's body.

"Some of it," Gabriel says. "And don't look so horrified. He doesn't deserve your pity."

"It doesn't matter what he's done, no one deserves that."

"If you had a full accounting," Damon Scott says, emerging from the shadows, "I think you would disagree. However, the stories aren't fit for polite company."

I take a step back, afraid to find out exactly how far gone he is. It's one thing to know the man hanging from rope is evil. Another to see the man I love, his beautiful smile, his hollow eyes.

He pauses, as if he doesn't want to frighten me. *Too late, too late.*

"Forty years ago they thought they could cure what was wrong with his brain." Damon waves a hand at the abandoned hospital. "That enough heat or electricity or water could shock the crazy out of him."

"That's barbaric," Avery gasps.

Gabriel examines the poker, its tip red and hot. "And ineffective."

"Then why are you doing it?"

He tosses the poker down to the dirty floor.

"I'm not trying to cure him."

"You're torturing him," she says, her voice thick with tears. "It's one thing to kill someone in self-defense. Even revenge. Another to hurt someone like this, to destroy them, to mutilate his body."

Gabriel looks as cold as Damon. As broken. "Have I shocked you again, little virgin?"

"Yes," she whispers.

I touch the back of her hand, my heart aching. I've only just found this family and it's already breaking apart. "He's trying to save you."

She looks at me, uncertain. "How?"

"Yes, how?" Jonathan Scott says, looking almost playful. All those years ago I thought it was Damon who looked like his father, who sounded like him, but now the tables have turned. Now it's Jonathan who looks eerily like his son, jovial and haunting. "Tell her how Gabriel Miller bought her and fucked her and keeps her locked away from the world, all in a desperate bid to save her pretty tits."

"Get them out of here," Gabriel mutters.

I'm not sure who he's talking about until Damon steps towards me.

I take a step back. It's Avery who says, "I'm not going anywhere."

"You really shouldn't see this," Gabriel says.

"It shouldn't be happening! You've caught him. You *have* him. You can turn him over to the cops."

"The chief of police is dear old Dad's drinking buddy," Damon says, his tone bored. "They liked to torture animals together while they watched the game on Sundays."

Avery gasps.

"Did I say animals?" Damon says, glancing at me with a dark expression. "Sometimes dogs. Sometimes girls. Anyone who would scream."

"Sometimes you," Avery whispers.

He looks sharply at her. "He doesn't deserve your compassion."

"Maybe not, but what about Gabriel? What do you think this is doing to him?"

"You can't save him, little virgin."

"You should get Penny out of here," Avery says. "She's been through enough."

He takes a step toward me. I back up, but he keeps coming. His hand grips my wrist.

"Come," he mutters, dragging me behind him.

"I guess I was useful, after all," I say as he leads me down the cracked path, taking me away from the mental hospital for the second time. It's a small improvement that I can walk this time around. I know without asking that it's not a coincidence.

"What?" he asks, his voice curt.

"I was the bait, after all," I say, my voice small. "Not the one you used to find your father. The one he used to find you."

Damon doesn't answer.

It's hard to say who actually won that battle. Damon may not be the one strung up by his wrists, his body tortured and raw, but his eyes look dead inside.

DAMON BRINGS ME to the diner, which is about the strangest thing that's happened to me in days. Which is really saying something. It's surreal to see the flickering overhead lights and the cracked linoleum that were once so familiar.

"Why are we here?" I manage to ask.

"You must be hungry."

"No."

"When's the last time you ate?"

I'm not sure I've actually eaten anything to-day. I was too nervous about the plan, too busy keeping an eye on Avery in case she tried to escape without me. "I'm not sure."

His smile is a perfect baring of teeth. "Then let's just say I'd like to feed you."

He holds the door open for me in a parody of chivalry.

If he were truly a gentleman, we wouldn't be in this place. It's where people go when they're tired and they can't be bothered to go anywhere else.

With a gallant sweep of his arm he gestures to the corner booth.

The same booth where Jonathan Scott once ordered pie. A coincidence?

Swallowing down my disgust I sit on the hard booth, trying not to think about who once sat here. I know a million people have been here since then. A million people before him. It doesn't stop the shiver that runs down my spine.

"Why didn't we go to Gabriel's house?" I ask, my voice low.

"This is closer," Damon says, which is true.

But not the whole truth. "I won't be going back there, will I?"

"Why would you? There's no threat to you anymore."

Jessica leaves the kitchen and sees us, her eyes wide. She grabs two mugs and a coffee pot from the counter, bringing them straight over. "What can I get you?" she asks, keeping her tone neutral. As if she doesn't know how huge it is that I'm here with him.

"We'll have a slice of pie," Damon says, his voice clipped.

My breathing speeds up. This doesn't feel coincidental. The same booth. The same order. Damon isn't making me prepare his coffee, but this still feels like history repeating.

"Are you sure that's all?" Jessica asks, her gaze meeting mine.

She's asking if I need help. The offer sends a needle through my heart. We both know there's not much she could do if I *did* need help, but it's sweet to have friends.

"That's all," I tell her, forcing a small smile.

When she leaves there's only silence. The muted shout of Ruth Mae as she gives Jackson grief. How many times have I heard those things? It feels so strange to be here, like I'm a puzzle piece that's gotten wet, the cardboard expanded. I don't quite fit anymore.

"How long were you in that place?"

"We staked it out for a week before he came back. There was a short struggle, but we had the upper hand."

"So you've been torturing him for two weeks?"

He looks at me sharply, as if surprised I would mention something so indelicate, despite the fact that he still smells faintly of something burnt. "And would have gone on longer, if you hadn't shown up."

"Am I supposed to apologize?" I ask, feeling defensive.

"No," he says, dismissing the idea. "That's not necessary."

I hate the tone he's using with me, like I'm beneath his notice or care. It's so far away from the low, seductive voice he gave me all those nights. But as much as his tone bothers me, his silence hurts worse. All the things he isn't telling me. Leaving me in the dark.

Stripping away my dignity, exactly like his father did in this very booth.

"What happens now?" I ask, digging my nails into my palms.

Neither of us have touched the coffee mugs.

Jessica returns, giving me a worried glance as she sets down a slice of pie. Blueberry this time. Neither of us acknowledge it. After a quick nervous look at Damon, she returns to the kitchen.

"You can go back to your life," Damon says, as casually as talking about the weather.

Once upon a time those words would have

been met with relief. Now I can't imagine anything more horrible. Not even green tiles and black water are worse than this. "What?"

"I've taken care of your father's other debts," he adds, like that's my only objection.

"No."

There's a weighted pause, as if Damon's giving me time to reflect on my disobedience. This is what he's become all those days torturing his father, becoming him. Losing that final battle.

"I don't believe you have a choice," he says lightly.

"You said I would be yours. Yours to keep."

"For as long as I want," he says agreeably. "Time's up."

It shouldn't be so hard to breathe outside the water. At least my gasp is silent, my pain private. "You said I would be yours to protect."

"And you're safe now. You can run back to your little boyfriend. What was his name? Brandon?"

"Brennan," I say, tears stinging my eyes.

"Right. I'm sure he would love to fix your intimacy issues and give you a couple babies. You can live happily ever after."

"That's not what I want," I say, my voice low.

"Oh, my sweet Penny. Where did you get the idea that matters?"

CHAPTER TWENTY-ONE

"**Y**OU HAVE TO eat something," Daddy says, pushing a dry hot dog in front of me.

I swear to God everyone wants me to eat, as if food can fix this gaping hole inside me. As if it has anything to do with the way my body has shifted and grown and *changed.*

The edge of the hot dog has turned white from being in the microwave too long. The ketchup has slid down the crack of the bun, forming a pool on the plate. Nothing about this is appetizing, even if I were hungry. Except that Daddy made this for me.

A hundred nights he was gone playing card games, leaving me to scrounge for food, to learn to work the stove before I really should have. All I'd wanted was *this*, a dry hot dog that he would make for me.

I force myself to take a bite. Somehow it tastes worse than it looks.

Chew. Swallow. Act like a person.

Daddy's eyes are wide with hope and worry.

"If you don't like it I can bring something else."

"No," I say, a little loud. "No, this is perfect. Thank you."

The truth is he's been nothing but supportive ever since Damon dropped me off at the door, like an errant lost puppy he was returning to its owner. Daddy fell over himself apologizing to me, swearing things would be different. At the time I had been too numb and too cold to even run through the ordinary thoughts—*don't believe him, Penny. It will only be worse when he gambles again.*

Except he didn't gamble again. Not in the three weeks I've been home.

That might not sound like much, but once upon a time it would have been a miracle.

Now it's a curiosity. A concern, even. Who is this man?

When I've eaten half the hot dog, I push the plate away. My stomach threatens to revolt if I don't stop. "When is the big game?" I finally bring myself to ask.

He freezes in the act of putting ketchup in the fridge. "What game?"

Guilt burns like acid inside me, because he looks so pained. So ashamed. I don't want to make him feel bad. That's how dark and twisted family makes you. You're desperate to console them even when they've hurt you.

"The game you used me to buy in."

He flinches. "I'm so sorry, Penny. I never should have done that. Your mother—"

There's a whirlpool inside me, a constant and wild swirl that's been there ever since Damon walked away from me. And for a moment, everything goes still. "What about her?"

"She would have killed me," he says, sitting down heavily at the kitchen table. His knee still bothers him, but he doesn't use the cane. It sits by the door instead, a wishful-thinking weapon in case Jonathan Scott comes back.

For so many years I tried not to think of Mama in that bathtub. And when I saw Jonathan Scott hanging from the ceiling of that mental hospital, I couldn't *stop* thinking of her. They didn't look alike, not in those moments, not before. There was only a kind of helpless self-destruction to both of them. They had not sunk to the bottom of the lake; they had both dived in head first.

"She wouldn't have cared," I say softly.

"Oh, Penny. What she did… she was sick. And I wasn't strong enough to help her."

Not while he was busy battling his own addiction. Not while he was making his own dive.

Maybe Damon Scott and I are destined to repeat history, each of us too wrapped up in our own pain to help the other swim. I already know I can't rely on him. Or Daddy.

Brennan came to see me three times now. He looked ashen the first two visits, unable to fully meet my eyes. I thought maybe he considered me damaged goods. He wouldn't have been wrong.

"You don't have to come again," I told him the third time, gently because I wasn't angry.

He glanced at me, his eyes wide with grief. "I'm not sure I can be your friend anymore."

The words startle me. "What?"

"I know you wanted that from me, so I didn't push. I didn't—but I did want more, Penny. I want that now. To marry you and make it so you never see Damon Scott again. Do you want that?"

I could have relied on him, but I couldn't hurt him that way. I couldn't lie.

No, the only person I can rely on is myself. "The poker game," I remind Daddy.

He shakes his head, fierce and quick. "Damon took over the game, after Jonathan Scott—" A cough that I'm not sure is a queasy stomach or genuine sickness. He hasn't been well. "After Jonathan Scott disappeared. He said all the previous buy-ins were now considered contributions to his father's funeral."

My eyes widen. "He can do that?"

A helpless shrug. "Someone could challenge him, but I doubt they'd survive long that way."

"Then it's over."

"It's over," he says firmly. "He's setting up another game, another buy-in, but I'm not interested. Okay, that's not entirely true. I'm interested, but I'm going to stay strong. Like I should have done a long time ago. There's no chance I'll enter."

Another game. *Another chance.* "We're going."

His face goes pale. "Penny, why? To watch? I shouldn't. I can't. Even though I'm trying to be strong... I have a ways to go. I'm afraid I'll slip back into that life. And if you're interested in Damon Scott, you should know—"

"I'm not," I say quickly, not wanting to hear one of the million reasons that would be dumb. Which reason would he pick to tell me? That the man is ten years older than me, gorgeous, wealthy, and could have any woman he wants? Or that he's a dangerous criminal?

Or maybe he would say what he means every time he pushes more food at me, his tone careful, his eyes filled with regret. That I'm damaged goods, after all. Ruined.

I put my hand on his. "I want to enter this. I want to play. Well, you'll play. I'll help."

He looks bewildered. "Why?"

"Because we'll split the pot."

"Money isn't a good reason," he says. "I should know."

"It's the only way I can control what happens to me. It's the only way I can be free."

Chapter Twenty-Two

I KNEW THE Den would be packed, but it's still shocking to see it lit up and sparkling, so different from how dark and bloody I saw it last. Yellow light spills from the door, which stands open. Two bouncers stand on either side, as large as professional football players. Maybe they actually *are* professional football players. They're wearing suits which had to have been custom made. No way does anything that broad in the chest and arms come off a rack.

They're checking names off a list.

Some of the people clutch a cream vellum invitation with calligraphy, as if to prove that they're allowed. Apparently their elegant gowns and tuxes wouldn't be proof enough. I'm sure no one gets in if their identity isn't confirmed.

"We won't get in," I say, my heart squeezing.

I knew it would be a bumpy road convincing Damon to let us play, hiding the counting and the signals, but it aches to be stopped so early. That game means college-level math classes and professional addiction therapy for Daddy. It means freedom from ever being bartered again.

"Let's try," Daddy says, but I know he's secretly relieved we'll be stopped.

He thinks Damon Scott is just as bad as his father. I tell him it's not true, but that sounds like a lie. He looked so much like Jonathan Scott at the end, his eyes more pale and shimmery than ever. Like a cold, unfeeling monster. And then he'd left me, his eyes as impassive and stone-black as the water in that pool.

Exactly the opposite of what Damon Scott had been to me.

"Penny," calls a feminine voice.

I turn to see Avery in a glittering gown that hugs her slender body. She looks like a celebrity stepping out of the limo. Gabriel emerges in a tux, growling about safety and letting him go first. The rough sidewalk could be a red carpet when they stroll over.

She grins at me. "You look lovely."

I glance down at my black dress. There are sequins on it, which is the only nod to fanciness I had. Manufactured sparkle. Fake gems. And the saddest part is that the dress isn't even mine. I borrowed it from Jessica. *Give me something that will help me blend in with rich people.*

"Thanks," I say weakly. "I'm not sure we'll get in."

"I didn't know you'd be here."

My confidence wavers. "I…I have to talk to Damon."

"Oh," she says, hooking her elbow in mine. "You can come in with us."

"There's security. And they look… strong."

"Gabriel will get us in," she says, sure of him with a serenity that makes me blush.

Gabriel leans forward and whispers a few words in one of the bouncer's ear. Then I'm ushered inside, Daddy following on our heels. One hurdle down. At least a hundred to go.

The crowd glitters in the large foyer, large gemstones sparkling from their necks, champagne glasses in their hands. Many of them turn to look at Gabriel Miller when we enter. Most of the women check him out. Some of the men, too. He cuts a handsome figure in his tux, his wild mane of hair and rare golden eyes compelling.

But only one man captures my attention, all the way in the back of the crowd, lurking in the shadows. Black eyes meet mine, glinting from the chandeliers.

Gabriel Miller is as bold as thunder, rumbling, unmistakable.

Damon Scott is lightning, so bright he'll blind you. They're both forces of nature but only one will kill you just to touch him. Only one will burn you in a flash.

Damon pushes through the crowd, more furious than I've ever seen him. "What are you doing here?"

The chatter stops almost completely, everyone watching us. Embarrassment turns my cheeks red. I don't belong here, but this is my only chance. "I'm with my father. He's playing tonight."

"Like hell he is," Damon says, glaring at Gabriel. "Did you bring them?"

"I took them in off the streets, if that's what you mean," Gabriel says in a slow drawl, clearly entertained by his friend's fury.

"We took a cab," I say, my fingers clenching together.

"Get out," Damon says, eyes on me.

Acid rises in my throat. This is it. More than the game is at stake here. We're at stake. Him. Me. Whatever twisted future we might have, when I'm a woman and he's a man. "I'll go," I whisper.

"Not you," he says sharply. "Everyone else."

There are gasps and whispers. A few drunken protests.

He glances at Gabriel. "Kick them out. Or let them play, for all I care. I'm done here."

With that he grasps my wrist, his grip firm but not bruising.

Despite his words I expect him to throw me out into the street. Or maybe take me to the private room with the small card table. What I don't expect is for him to pull me up the stairs. I already know what's here. I've been here before, carried in his arms. His bedroom.

There must be other rooms up here. We're going to one of them.

But I know, even before we stop outside his bedroom. Before he crosses the threshold, taking me with him. Before he locks the door with an old-fashioned skeleton key.

There's only one place he would take me tonight.

"All right," he says, his tone casual. "Let's play."

"I want to play in the big game," I say, my voice shaking.

"You don't think I'm big enough?" he asks, his voice mocking.

"The grand prize. That's what I need to win."

"I thought you weren't playing. It was dear old Dad who's going to play, right? With you as his wager. Surely you weren't going to help him in any illegal manner."

My hands are shaking. My whole body shakes. I'm an earthquake in the form of a young woman. "Fine, then I'll play myself. I'll be my own wager."

"So that you can count cards?" he asks softly. "That isn't allowed."

"How will you know?" I say, my throat dry.

"We don't have to know," he says. "That's what you don't seem to understand. We only have to *think* you're counting cards, and that's enough to break your knees."

I flinch. "Then I won't count them."

"You won't be able to stop yourself. You and I both know that."

He's right about that. I won't be able to stop any more than I can stop breathing or existing or wanting this man I shouldn't. "Then I really can't play."

"Oh, I didn't say that. We'll definitely play. Not in the big game, though. We'll have a private one, you and I." Walking over to a small circular table with two chairs, he pulls something from his pocket. A deck of cards, the box unopened. It lands on the gleaming wood surface. "Strip poker."

Shock renders me speechless. "What?"

"Strip," he says, pausing enough to make me flush. "Poker. You've heard of it, haven't you?"

Of course I've heard of it.

The boys are always asking the girls to play at parties. It's not really a game. Not a real wager. The only goal is to get undressed. To find an empty room upstairs and have sex.

"No," I say.

He nods. "That's perfectly fine. If you don't want to play, you don't have to."

My heart stops. "Wait."

"Yes?" he asks, all distant politeness.

"I want to play. But not strip poker. Something else." I'm desperate, knowing I'm already beaten. "Blackjack. Rummy. Anything."

He smiles, but it's not sweet. It's a cold smile, beautiful in its sparseness. "Take it or leave it, baby."

All of this is wrong. We should be downstairs. I should be on the sidelines, helping Daddy move to the next round. Damon should be running the show like a ringmaster, casually debonair. Controlling the whole room with a calculated smile.

Then again there's something hard and right about this moment. The two of us alone, the same way we began. There's no lake near us, only the shared nightmare of water. No trees around us except the walls of the Den.

"I'll take it."

"Have a seat," he says, pulling out a chair.

It feels ominous, that invitation.

I sit in the wooden chair with its leather cushion anyway. Nowhere near as heavenly as the one downstairs, but just as lush, just as expensive. The sequins on my dress pull against the leather as I scoot into place.

"Now," he says, taking his seat opposite me. "For the bet. What shall we wager? Something large. You were concerned about size, I recall."

A flush heats my cheeks. "That's why I'm doing this. So I don't have to worry about Daddy gambling again. So I don't have to be afraid."

He hesitates for one sweet moment, as if he might bring us to a stop. Then he continues on as if he never stopped, unpackaging the fresh deck, shuffling them quickly.

With a small flourish he sets the deck down. "Cut it."

I pick a random spot and cut the deck in half. He folds it over.

"I accept your terms," he says softly. "If you win you get freedom from worry. From fear. No one will ever be able to use you against your will again."

Does that mean money? How much money? I'm almost afraid to ask, because the truth is no amount of money will make me stop being afraid. No amount of money will stop the nightmares. It's not money that will save me—it's power.

"What would you win?" I ask, not sure this question is any better.

"Your father," he says, surprising me. "He stays with me. He disappears."

My mouth drops open. "What?"

"Don't look so surprised. You should even be glad. Either way you're free of him, of the gambling and the lies. The weakness. That's what you wanted, isn't it?"

In this moment what I want is...*him.* Whether he's the wild boy or the perfectly handsome Damon Scott, he's always been kind to me. Playful and brooding, his touch in turns coaxing and commanding. He only turned cruel once he tortured his father.

Once he *became* his father, which was all Jonathan Scott wanted.

"What would you want with Daddy?" I say, my voice trembling.

"Does it matter what I do with him? He

didn't ask questions when he used *you* as his bet into the game. I suppose he didn't need to ask questions." Dark eyes run over my body, as if he can see through the sequins and the thin black fabric. As if he sees my heart beating rapid-fire under my ribs. "It's fairly obvious what we would do with you."

I understand then what this is. A test of my will.

He has to put something on the line, something I would hate to lose. And I almost stop. Because who am I to bet my father's life? Then again, who was he to bet mine? If I do this, I'll become just as bad as him. Maybe that's the point.

Making me turn into my father the way he turned into his.

"Fine," I say.

"Three rounds," he says, dealing the cards.

My first hand starts weak—nothing with a queen high. With new cards I end up with a king, which his three of a kind queens easily beats. He wins the first round.

Staring at him, I swallow. That means I have to strip. I have to take off a piece of clothing. With shaking hands I remove a red bangle Jessica loaned me from my wrist.

He laughs softly. "Does that count?"

"Doesn't it?" I ask, arching my eyebrow, daring him to argue.

I win the second round with two pairs, relief pouring over me.

His eyes glint. "What should I remove?"

I shrug, expecting him to take off his watch. His shoes. There are so many innocuous things he could remove on such a finely dressed man. The only thing missing from him is his jacket, which he removed when we entered the room.

Standing, he reaches for the button at his collar. Oh God, he's going to remove his shirt. My skin suddenly feels prickly and too tight. The tendons in his hands move subtly as he undoes each button, revealing a sliver of golden skin and a hint of dark hair.

When the buttons are finished he pulls the hem from his pants, letting the two halves of white linen hang open. His masculine figure takes my breath away. Power, exactly the way I dreamed about.

Then his hands move to his wrists, where he works at the cufflinks.

They drop onto the table in front of me. Curious because they aren't sterling silver or even gold. They're this deep copper color, blackened at the edges.

Realization washes over me, as potent and clear as an ocean wave.

It's a penny. A real penny that has been attached to a bracket, melded to make this cufflink that he wears on his body. I pick one up and find it warm.

My gaze rises to meet his. "Where is this from?"

I already know the answer, but it still makes me shiver to hear him say, "They're two of the breadcrumbs you left me. So I never forget."

From the haunted look I know he never would have.

It might be a memory, but it's also a punishment. Is that what I mean to him?

He shrugs his powerful shoulders, letting the fabric fall to the floor. The only other time I saw him shirtless was when I had just been attacked. I couldn't look close. Only now can I see his tattoos clearly. And only now can I see the scars between them. Elaborate scrolls and dragon scales. They're beautiful, and they almost, *almost* distract from the silvery lines between them. Scars.

I stand, sick to my stomach. "He did that to

you."

"Are you surprised?" he asks, his voice low and taunting. "Are you disgusted by me?"

He sounds so casual, but I know that's not real. He hates them. Hates them so much he's covered them up with miles of ink—still never enough. How many people have seen him this way? How many women have actually seen him naked?

How many suits does he wear to hide his past?

I reach out a hand. "Damon, please."

He turns away with a rough sound. "We aren't here to talk about my father. We're here to play a final hand for yours."

There's bile in my throat. I'm sick looking at him, how beautiful he is, how broken. Except he holds himself away from me, his body straight, muscles tight.

Reluctantly I sit down across from him.

My voice comes out halting. More sincere than I've ever been with him. Tears prick my eyes. "I'm sorry. That I sent you back there. I was sorry every day of my life."

"Don't be," he says softly. "I was never sorry I did that."

"And now?"

He deals the final hand. "I guess we'll find

out."

The cards look like snakes to me. Deadly. Poisonous. I don't want to touch them. They're the root of everything ugly in my life—gambling and risk. Money.

How could anything this dark actually help me?

Of course the slick coating on the thin cards feels the same in my hands when I pick them up. There's nothing different about the cards. I'm the one who's changed.

A straight flush. An incredible hand, minus one card.

It seems impossible. I have to keep my eyes down so he doesn't see my excitement. My nervousness. Because this can't be real. It's like I'm dreaming the six of hearts. The seven, the eight, and the ten. The last card doesn't suit, I'm hovering on the edge of a precipice.

I push the fifth card down and receive a new one.

I'm sure fangs will sink into my skin if I reach for it. Poison will spread through my veins. *Calm down,* I tell myself. *It's just a game.* But I learned a long time ago that it's more than that. It's hunger and it's pain. Or it can be survival.

My hand is strangely steady as I reach for the

last card. Even if it bites me I have to know. I lift the card, struggling to breathe. Struggling to see. Adrenaline blurs the nine. The hearts. I got it. *The straight flush.*

A beautiful, perfect hand.

Elation runs through me. In that moment I know exactly why Daddy gambles. It's impossible not to love this, not to *become* this wild triumphant creature. Intellect may make us human, but this desperate desire for risk keeps us animal.

Damon's eyes glint dark in the lamplight. "You look pleased," he says.

And he doesn't look worried.

Because he wants me to win? Or because he knows he can beat me.

I put down my cards. He doesn't flinch. Doesn't react beyond a genial nod of his head, acknowledging a good hand. "Well played, baby genius. Not good enough, but still. A very good showing."

One thud in my chest. Another. Painfully slow, time crawling now.

"How?"

He tosses down his cards with casual superiority. A royal flush. The only thing that could have beaten my cards, almost. And nearly impossible. The odds…

God, the odds.

Randomness doesn't play favorites. That ace of spades is as likely to appear as any other card. The king, the queen. Except when you put the odds together, they multiply. They become infinitely smaller. Like in calculus, they approach zero—never quite reaching it.

My breath comes short. "You cheated."

He laughs. "How do you know? Did you see me do something?"

My mind races, a hundred numbers swirling around, a thousand of them clamoring for attention. It's really the simplest one that has the answer. The cards that we played. My hand of nothing, queen high. His three of a kind, queens.

"The queens. They've all been played."

Which means the one sitting in front of us right now, it doesn't belong in the deck. Whether he modified the deck beforehand or whether he used sleight of hand to insert it, that queen doesn't belong in this deck. And I'm willing to bet the entire hand is fake.

"I don't see how you can prove it," he says, his voice mocking.

I stand up. "If you're cheating the game doesn't count."

He stands too, reaching for his shirt. Putting

it back on, like armor. Covering up the scars of the past and all that beautiful vulnerability. "Oh, the game most definitely counts. Your father is forfeit. And you, my sweet Penny, are free to go."

THE END

THANK YOU!

I hope you loved reading Damon and Penny's emotional book. Find out the conclusion of their duet with the epic full-length novel THE QUEEN. Order it now!

Don't forget to sign up for my VIP reader list where you'll get exclusive giveaways, free books, and new release alerts.

Have you read the USA Today bestselling Endgame trilogy? If not, be sure to start with THE PAWN. A virgin auction has never been this dangerous…

And you'll love the sensual, dark, and dangerous USA Today bestselling Stripped series. The prequel novella Tough Love is available to download at all online book retailers. By the way, this is the series where Ivan and Candy first appear.

And don't miss the rough + sexy bestselling Chicago Underground series, starting with ROUGH! *I never thought a man that rough could be my prince…*

And if you're looking for something sexy and sweet and romantic, you can fall in love with this modern fairy tale retelling! You can find the first part Beauty Touched the Beast, at all retailers now.

I appreciate your help in spreading the word, including telling a friend. Reviews help readers find books! Please leave a review on your favorite book site.

You can also join my Facebook group, Skye Warren's Dark Room, for exclusive giveaways and sneak peeks of future books.

This edition of THE KING includes bonus content. ORCHARD is a *very dark* story of what happened to Penny the night of her attack, as told by Jonathan Scott.

ORCHARD

THE GIRL NOTICES me when I walk in the door, heralded by the sad chime of a cracked bell. The stiffness of her spine betrays her. I don't think she recognizes me. If she did she'd slip out the back door, Mary Janes slapping the pavement as she ran home. But she recognizes power.

I take a seat in the corner, sinking onto a vinyl bench with the stuffing peeking out of the seams. The Italian shoes I'm wearing could buy out the mortgage on this godforsaken diner, but no one else wants it. The same way a farmer can look at a dry plot of land, I see possibility.

And the ripest fruit is the girl, her cheeks pink from exertion, wisps of blond hair curling over her temple. Every man in this place watches her as she bustles and sweats to earn every two-dollar tip. It's the closest they come to making her stroke their cocks, having her fetch watered-down coffee, again and again.

She breezes over, mug and pot in hand, pouring before I've ordered. "What can I get you?"

I nod toward the glass platter on the counter. "What kind of pie?"

"Peach."

Of course. "I'll have that."

She manages a brief smile, not quite meeting my eyes, before bustling back to get me a slice.

Yes, I can see why this derelict diner stays open in the war zone that is west Tanglewood. If I only had ten dollars in my pocket, I wouldn't buy a blow job from the whore on the corner. I'd make this girl scurry back and forth, back and forth.

I have much more than ten dollars to my name.

And she will do a lot more to earn it.

She returns with a slice on a white ceramic plate and a fork. It's obscene, the way the fruit has slid from the cuts, the glisten of sweet syrup. The way strips of flesh-colored crust drape over the filling.

"What's your name?"

She hesitates only a moment. "Penny."

Her full name is Penelope Margaret Hartford. Such a dignified name for a baby born addicted to drugs from her bitch of a mother, her father in prison before she drew her first ragged breath. "How long have you been working here, Penny?"

She hesitates a little longer this time. Eventually she'll give me everything—her body, her sanity. But I want to see how far I can push first.

"Two years."

Two years would have made her fifteen years old. I've owned Mel's Diner since before that, but I never came here. Never saw her. And that's a damn shame. How sweet would it have been to see her cheeks rounded with youth, her knees knobby?

Fifteen would have made her underage for what I have planned. That's also a damn shame. I prefer to break every rule that exists, prefer anarchy to order. I would have fucked her peachy little cunt when she was underage. Illegal. Naturally, I'll still do it. A little more coercion, a little more twisted desire, will make her just as delicious.

I tip my head toward the cup of coffee, exactly where she left it before. "I prefer two creams. Three sugars."

She pauses, uncertain whether to shove the small container of watery creams and old sugar toward me. That's what a busy diner waitress would do for a normal customer, but I'm far from normal.

In fact, I don't prefer this weak excuse for

coffee at all, but I want to see her dither. I want to see her weigh whatever tip this rich stranger might give against the gas bill at home, weigh her natural desire to obey against the sexual undertone of my request.

After a moment, she reaches for the ceramic container. Slender fingers dig out two tiny cups of cream. Three paper packets of sugar. Her hands are shaking as she pours them into the mug.

White nondairy creamer swirls into the center, embraced by the black. Sugar sinks to the bottom.

I make no move to hold the spoon, to stir them into the coffee. There's a surface kind of strength that men seek—always controlling with their hands, their bodies. Even their words. God, the sweet pressure around my cock as she obeys me without a single sound, as she rushes to please me without my even issuing a command. It's inherent between us, my authority, her obeisance. She can feel it, even if she doesn't understand it.

She picks up the spoon and stirs until the coffee becomes a warm brown, swirling around silver.

"Is that—" She catches herself, wondering why she's doing this for me, most likely. Wondering what hold I have over her. "Is that everything?"

Not even close. "What time do you get off?"

How many times has someone asked her this? If a man is young and handsome, it means he's asking her on a date. I'm betting plenty have tried. I'm not young. At least twenty-five years her senior. And I'm definitely not handsome. The last escort I fucked said I look like the devil himself. She had my fingerprints bruised on her neck, so that might have influenced her opinion.

A small shake of her head, almost as if she's gathering herself. "That's not really—"

"Appropriate? I'm rarely appropriate."

"I'll come back and check on you in a little bit."

"I'd rather you sit down with me."

She takes a step back. "Please stop."

What a good girl, protecting herself. Too bad it won't help.

I watch as she ducks into the kitchen. Checking on a meal, or hiding from me? When she emerges, she avoids my side of the diner completely, delivering food and handing out checks without making eye contact. Such a little press into her boundaries, such a lovely display of vulnerability. There's so much more for us to explore.

I drop a hundred-dollar bill on the table,

leaving the coffee and the pie untouched. She'll think about me for the rest of her shift. For the rest of the week. She'll look over her shoulder for me.

I'm a farmer in this concrete land, money my tool, fear a steady fall of rain.

And very soon, I'll pick the sweetest peach for myself.

DARKNESS COATS THE city like sweet dew, nourishing and slick. It's my favorite time to walk the streets, when no one recognizes me. Unless I want them to.

I'm six steps behind little Penny, cloaked in shadow. She knows someone follows her, but she doesn't know who. Does my face come to mind— silver eyes and black hair? Does she know which wolf stalks her? On the west side of Tanglewood, it could be a nameless rapist. Not Jonathan Scott, the amoral businessman who owns most of this cracked concrete.

My footsteps echo off the bricks on either side.

She speeds up, her shoes slapping the wet pavement. Her shoulders hunch down, instinctively making her smaller. She's already so petite, body thin and undernourished. Except for her tits and ass, a red flag to bulls like me. Her body can't help but be fertile. She can't help but attract me.

Poor Penny. She can't help being so fun to break.

Around the corner toward her house, she spurs into a run. My steps lengthen to their usual stride, but I don't chase after her. Not quickly. Not when she's running straight into the trap I've set. The entire tenement is a maze made for small people, powerless people.

Her door is shut, the lock turned.

I knock. There's a key in my pocket the property manager gave me. I'd rather be let inside. The devil wants an invitation.

The door opens a crack, yanked short by a brass chain. A wide, fearful brown eye takes me in. "You."

"Me," I say agreeably. "May I come inside?"

"Who are you?"

The man who's going to strip you down, layer by layer. Until I get to your beating heart. "The owner of this building."

Her eyes narrow. "You're not the super."

"He works for me."

"How do I know I can trust you?"

My cock twitches at being challenged, even

this small amount. My reputation is so absolute, my power so replete that I rarely find this— especially from a girl so small.

"You definitely can't trust me. Run and tell your daddy that Jonathan Scott is here."

She shuts the door and turns the deadbolt with a squeak. I hear soft voices through the thin walls but not what they're saying. I can imagine it well enough. *Jonathan Scott? Are you serious? Open the fucking door. Let him in before he kicks it in.*

I would never do something so crass. I became powerful so that I could direct people instead of the other way around. The door opens about sixty seconds later.

A breathless Penny swings open the door. "Come in."

An older man hobbles inside, leaning on both the wall and a single crutch. His leg is wrapped in denim, a poor man's cast. Someone who can't afford health care. "Mr. Scott," he says, cheeks ruddy, eyes bright with pain and fear. "What can we do for you?"

"Please sit down, George. Don't strain yourself on my account."

He hesitates, clearly preferring to stand even as his balance wavers. No one wants to sit down around an animal baring its teeth. Penny helps him to a lumpy plaid armchair. Such a good daughter.

I do him the favor of sitting across from him, on an old corduroy sofa. It's a courtesy I can extend since I'll have my cock in his daughter tonight. "I understand my son has been to visit you."

Fear glistens over the man's eyes. He glances at his broken leg. "I told him we'd get it. I swear."

I shake my head, disappointed. "Don't lie to me. There's no way for you to get ten thousand dollars. Little Penny could serve a hundred pies a day, and you'd never be able to pay."

"Stop it," Penny says, brown eyes flashing. "Leave him alone."

Like biting into a peach, the slight crisp, the hint of tartness beneath the sweetness. Heat courses through my body, rare for someone so jaded, so fucking experienced. Almost an old man, really.

"I could," I say idly. "Leave him alone, I mean. If you want me to."

A hard swallow. "What do you mean?"

"Ten thousand dollars." I pull out an envelope thick with hundred dollar bills. Just like the one I left her on the Formica table in the diner. I cock my head, studying her. "Would you like this,

Penny?"

George looks concerned. "No, leave her out of this. She didn't have nothing to do with it."

"You'll have to give the money to Damon yourself. Do you think you could manage that? Or would you gamble again, hoping to turn it into twenty or thirty thousand?"

"I'll make sure he gets it," Penny says with a worried glance at her daddy.

"You won't."

She doesn't want to ask. She has no choice. "Why not?"

"You'll be with me."

"No!" George says, struggling to heave himself up. An involuntary sound of pain fills the cramped apartment as he leans too much on his leg. "You can't do this."

He knows it's already done. He should have known that when I showed up at the door. Maybe he did. Maybe he sent his little girl to the door knowing it would be the last time.

"It's up to you," I say, smiling at her.

An impossible choice. A dirty old man with a taste for sweetness. Her lips firm. "You're a monster."

Fuck, I almost come in my pants. "That's right," I murmur. "Fight me."

"How dare you do this?"

"Offer you money? Well, sure, call the cops. Tell them how horrible I am for paying your daddy's debts."

"Aren't the police in your pockets?"

"Or you can take your chances with Damon Scott. He has quite a reputation." I glance at George's leg. "I suppose you're already familiar with it. What did he promise to take next?"

A furtive glance at his daughter is the only answer I need. Damon is my son, after all.

"Tick tock," I say softly. "Would you like the money?"

She looks to her daddy in that trusting, hopeful way a child does. Of course, her father has no comfort to offer. He can't even meet her eyes. That's the way Damon looked at me once. I didn't comfort him either.

"I'll do it," she says between clenched teeth.

I stand and leave the room without another word. The money remains on the cheap cushion where I left it. Her footsteps chase me down the hallway.

"Wait." She's breathless. "I'm coming."

I beat her down the uneven stairs and into the night. Only on the street do I let her catch up. "I don't wait for you, little girl. That's not how this works."

She bites her lip, clearly holding back some retort. The fire in her burns, where for too many years I felt numb. "Okay. I'll be good. I swear."

"Do you really think Daddy is going to use the money to pay off the debt?"

Large brown eyes look up at the building behind me. That's the true monster, its bones rotting wood, its skin crumbling concrete. Glassy eyes stare out, unblinking as it eats people up. There's no way her father will give the money to Damon. He'll gamble it away, ending up in more debt. It's a sickness.

The glimmer of hope in her eyes is a stroke to my cock.

"He knows what I'm giving up."

"Do you?"

Her eyes narrow, fierce with righteous anger. "You want to have sex with me."

"Wrong."

Even she knows that will be worse. Suspicion. Fear she tries to hide. "What, then?"

"I want to break you down into parts—into hope and despair. Into love and fear. I want to consume your humanity, feast on you, until there's nothing left but a small, jagged core at the center."

She should be afraid, and she is. More than that, she's defiant.

I knew I chose the best piece.

"Why?"

I laugh softly. "Do you ever think about how mechanical sex is? Men so desperate for something warm and wet to fuck. A purely physical sensation. We might as well be automatons."

"Not you," she says with a hint of bitterness.

It would be better if I only wanted to rape her. She knows that much.

"I learned to block out physical sensations as a child." I believe in honesty, in exposure. Secrets are weakness. "Pain. Sex. Hunger. They only touch our bodies. Not our minds."

She looks horrified. "What happened to you?"

I hold out my hand. "Come along."

It may as well be a snake, my fingers its fangs. "You're insane."

"No, little peach. I'm the only sane one in a world full of rabid animals." I have endless patience as I leave my hand outstretched. Mercy is important. Mercy to a girl who'll be broken soon enough.

She trembles as she puts her palm against mine.

I squeeze in comfort. I'm not a heartless man.

We take a long walk through the back alleys of the west side. Five blocks south and two west. The sign for the Midtown Asylum has long since crumbled, leaving only a large, plantation-style building. If the west side of Tanglewood is my orchard, then this building is the barrel of bruised fruit. It will be mashed and strained. Still useful for its indelible flavor, but no longer bearing the same colors.

On either side, there are houses falling down. I could repair them. Or maybe rent them as they are, to people desperate enough for a leaky roof. But I prefer the privacy. There's no one else on this street.

I have mansions and compounds scattered across Tanglewood, shows of wealth and of strength. They're fine for me to visit, to use like a simple man fucks a slick cunt. Temporary relief.

This is the only place I ever feel human.

I hear her indrawn breath before the lock has turned.

Pictures spread over the floor. The insides of senators' houses. The interiors of city hall. Windows into our twisted little world. I haven't hidden any of them from her—like I said, I believe in honesty.

"The desk," I tell her, hanging my coat on a

hook.

She takes a step forward. A soft moan of denial. "You watched me."

Her little bedroom with its faded quilt. The place she peeled off her cheap waitress uniform. The bed she slept in. "Sometimes at night, I'd hear you breathe faster. See your hand moving under the covers. It's so beautiful, the way you love yourself."

Her eyes are wide. Expression solemn. "I'm not leaving here, am I?"

"Not alive." Maybe she'd be breathing. Maybe she wouldn't.

Her mind would be cracked beyond repair.

It's inevitable that she would run, like a hand shrinking back from fire. She sprints for the door, her hand on the knob before I catch her slender body in my arms. It's a thrill to toss her onto the ground, to climb on top of her back. I do love when they run. That's the animal side of me. Sometimes I'm feral too.

The difference is I have a bigger goal. A better one.

I stroke her cheek with the backs of my fingers. "Lovely peach. So sweet."

She fights me, thrashing on the ground. Beating the concrete with her fists. "You're disgusting."

"Yes," I breathe. "You see it now. It's hard wearing suits. Wearing authority and power. The way people look at me—reverence. Fear. Not you."

It only takes a moment to open my pants, to push up the thin fabric of her skirt. To pull aside her panties. My cock notches against her puckered hole, and she freezes. "Wait," she says. "Wait, wait, wait."

"That's right," I whisper. "Beg."

Hands clench into fists. All that courage. "Don't do it. Not like this."

"On the floor. Held down like an animal. Looking at the face of the man you'll grow to love." I may taste her first, but she's a gift. A gesture of paternal love. The sweetest fruit for the very best son.

Damon looks so much like me. Younger, of course. Kinder.

My face will haunt her nightmares. She'll be terrified of him. That's my gift to him—her fear.

I plunge into her, ripping a scream from her throat. Her back muscles spasm around my cock, stretching and fighting the intrusion. My cock aches from entering her dry. What bliss. I press my face against the top of her head and breathe deep. She still smells like grease and stale coffee from the diner. Perfect.

From the side, I can see her face scrunched in pain. Tears leak down her cheeks.

"Watch," I say, nudging deeper with my cock. Did she think this was as hard as I could fuck her? I'm showing tenderness now. She glances back at me, still subsumed with the physical pain.

I reach to my back pocket and pull out my phone. It only takes a few clicks. The feed pulls up on the screen. There's her father, blowing the ten thousand dollars on useless bets.

Her sob fills my ears, a sweeter music than grunts and groans ever could be.

"You'll save that little cunt for someone special," I whisper into her ear. "Someone you love as much as me. I won't fuck you there."

"I hate you," she whispers, voice thick. In a thick hock, she spits. It lands on the phone screen, glistening and foamy. "I hate you, I hate you."

What she doesn't realize is that it hurts me at first. No lube. No saliva. But as I saw in and out of her, she lubricates with blood. That makes it the best place to fuck a woman. Or a man. A test of character.

Nature's gift to the powerful creatures.

Damon doesn't see that. He still likes to fuck

a slick, swollen cunt. He likes to make a woman spasm around his cock—in pleasure instead of pain. That makes him weak, no matter how many legs he breaks. What kind of father would I be if I didn't fix that?

Honestly, she's a mess.

I pull out and grasp my cock, pink and dark from her blood. One stroke, two. I aim toward the gaping hole, bright red and pulsing blood. I pump my cock until milky semen spurts across her pretty ass.

It's almost emotional, looking at her wound in the place I became a man.

I stand and fix my clothes, picking up the phone from where I dropped it. Exposure. I snap a picture of her. A few, because I want to make sure the lighting is just right. I've spent enough time preparing the piece, I should make the most of it.

Then I grasp her by the hair and drag her down a hallway. Third room on the right.

The Recreation room. A pool built for someone who wanted the crazy to exercise. Maybe even have fun. A metal grate lid added to keep people from falling in. It has a different purpose now.

Her feet scrabble for purchase on the broken

tiles. She can't fight the pull. Such beautiful blond strands. They look delicate framing her flushed face, but they aren't. They're strong. Like her. A wonderful leash with which to pull her into hell.

The hole gapes in the center of the room, black and dank.

She swings wildly in a punch that lands on my side. A very nice attempt, but not enough. I push her into the pit. The sound of her fall echoes against the walls. Six feet. Far enough to break something. She slips as she tries to stand, the concrete sides slick with mildew.

"Don't worry," I murmur. "This will help you, too."

What if he doesn't come? Then he would be more heartless than I am, and wouldn't that be sweet? A truly proud moment as a father. I think he'll come. He'll hate her. She'll fear him.

I turn the faucet on the wall, and water pours from a small steel pipe into the pit. She screams when she realizes what will happen. It will take a long time, but eventually, the pit will be full of water. The metal grate I slide over the top will keep her inside.

As it rises, she'll have to kick to stay afloat. Ultimately, she'll cling to the metal grate, her fingers through the holes, desperately sucking in air through the top. And then her arms will tire. Her mind will dull. The heroic Damon Scott will come for her, possibly. He might even come in time.

How long will she survive down there?

What will be left of her mind if she does?

"Please, no," she begs. She's really lovely like this, desperate and clawing.

I almost wish that I could keep her. Almost. "Don't panic," I say, chiding. "You'll only lose your head."

Tears stream down her cheeks. "Don't do this to me. I'll do anything, anything."

"You'll do everything, lovely peach."

"I'll make the money back. Work in the clubs. For sex. Anything. Don't do this to me. *Please.*"

Desperation is an aphrodisiac. I knew that, which was partly why I had to fuck her first. It doesn't stop my cock from growing hard again. "Do you know, when I first got here, they still did lobotomies. How barbaric is that?"

"*This* is barbaric," she half cries, half screams. "Let me out. Oh my God, let me out of here."

The water is already at her knees. "They did many cruel things, but not this. This was beautiful. I fought it first. That's the weakness inside us. It's a gift to make you stronger."

She backs up in the water, back against the corner, eyes wide with horror.

"Oh, I almost forgot." I pull up the picture on my phone and start a text to Damon. He doesn't have this number. It's one of many burner phones. Anonymous. Untraceable.

On impulse, I add a heart emoji. It makes me smile. He probably doesn't know I know how to use those. His old man. I may be a little tradition-al, but I can learn. I hit *Send*.

Only a second passes before he calls back.

I shove the phone into my pocket. We don't need to speak. He's my son. Our connection goes deeper than words. He'll know from the picture where she is. After all, this is where I made Damon stronger. The world is a cruel, dark place. I wanted him to be ready for it.

It feels a little melancholy to leave her there, the sweet fruit and the familiar barrel. God, even the smell of antiseptic lingers in the air decades later. I breathe in the scent for comfort.

Strange to realize I want the girl for myself. How I could torment her. In one of my mansions, using every room, every piece of ominous equipment. No clothes. Little food. Those beautiful, large brown eyes, full of fury. She's almost too good for him.

I pause with my hand on the doorknob, looking back down the hallway. Faintly, the water babbles, a peaceful sound like a brook. I'm watering her like a fucking plant. Making her grow.

And isn't that why farmers work so hard? To pass down the land to their sons?

It doesn't matter if I want to keep her. I can still feel the tight muscles of her asshole tearing around my cock. Still feel her hair in my fist. I want to consume her a hundred times. And then again.

My sacrifice doesn't matter.

She serves a bigger purpose—a family legacy.

Thank you for reading Orchard!

Jonathan Scott is a character in the Endgame series, which begins with The Pawn and continues in The Knight. I hope you'll try this dark + sexy virgin auction series!

"Skye Warren's THE PAWN is a triumph of intrigue, angst, and sensual drama. I was clenching everything. Gabriel and Avery sucked me in from the first few paragraphs and never let go."

– New York Times bestselling author Annabel Joseph

"Gabriel Miller is the perfect alpha, leaving you reeling as his dominance, power, and unexpected tenderness creates the ideal mixture. Five glowing stars."

– New York Times bestselling author Aleatha Romig

Turn the page for an excerpt from Tough Love…

Excerpt from Tough Love

THE MOON SITS high above the tree line. Somewhere beyond those woods is an electric fence. And beyond that is an entire city of people living and working and *loving* each other. I may as well be on the moon for how close I am to them.

A guard walks by my window at 10:05 p.m. Right on time.

I wait a few minutes until he's out of earshot; then I flip the latch. From there it's quick work to push up the pane with its bulletproof glass. I broke the lock a year ago. And almost every night since then I've sneaked down the ornate metal trellis—like a thief, stealing a moment to myself.

The grass is still damp from the rain, the ground beneath like a sponge, sucking me in. I cross the lawn, heart beating against my chest. I know exactly where the guards are on their rounds. I know exactly where the trip wires are that will set off the alarms. My father is too busy in his office to even glance outside.

SKYE WARREN

The office I broke into this morning.

I breathe a sigh of relief when I reach the pool. I'm still out in the open, but the bright underwater lights make it hard to see anything on the patio. They make it hard to see me as I curve around the edge and reach the pool house.

The door opens before I touch the handle. "Clara," comes the whisper.

I can't help but smile as I slip into the dark. Giovanni always opens the door for me. It's like some old-world chivalry thing, even though we're just two kids sneaking around. At least, that's how everyone treats me. Like a kid. But when I'm with him, I feel less like a girl, more like a woman.

He looks out the door for a beat before shutting and locking it. "Are you sure no one saw you?"

"You're such a worrywart, Gio." I let myself fall onto the couch, facing up.

"If your father ever found out…"

We'd be in so much trouble. My father is a member of the mob. Giovanni's father is a foot soldier who works security on the grounds. Both our dads are seriously dangerous, not to mention a little unhinged. I can't even think about how bad it would be if they caught us sneaking around after dark.

I push those thoughts away. "Did you bring it?"

Reluctantly, Giovanni nods. He gestures to the side table, where a half-full bottle of Jack Daniels gleams in the faint light. "Did you?"

I reach into the pockets of my jeans and pull out two cigars. I hold them up and grin. "Didn't even break a sweat."

He rolls his eyes, but I think he's relieved. "This was a bad idea."

"It was my idea," I remind him, and his cheeks turn dark.

Of course the little homework assignment was my idea. I'm the one ridiculously sheltered up in my room with the tutors and the gilded locks. Fifteen years old and I've never even been out to the movies. Giovanni gets to go to regular school. He's too young to get inducted, but I know he gets to be at some of the sit-ins.

"I just want to try them," I say. "I'm not going to get addicted or anything."

He snorts. "More likely you'll get a hangover. How are you going to explain puking to your padre?"

"Honor will cover for me." My sister always covers for me. She takes the brunt of my father's anger. Ninety-nine percent of the time, I love the way she protects me. But one percent of the time, it feels like a straitjacket. That's why I started coming to the pool house. And I'm glad I did. This is where I met Giovanni.

He examines the cigar, eyes narrowed.

"How do you even light it?" I ask. I've seen my father do it a hundred times, but I'm still not clear on how the whole thing doesn't just catch fire. Isn't it made from dried plants?

He puts the cigar to his lips experimentally. It looks strange seeing his full lips around something I've mostly seen my father use. Then he blows out a breath, miming how it would be. I imagine white smoke curling in front of his tanned skin.

"They don't let you use them when they do?" I ask.

He gives me a dark look. I'm not supposed to talk about the side jobs he does for his father. "I mostly sit in a corner and hope no one notices me. It's boring."

"If it's boring, then why won't you talk about it?" I know it's not a good thing to be noticed by men like our father, to be groomed by them, but sometimes that seems better than being ignored. I'm the younger one. And a girl. And there are rumors that I'm not even my father's legitimate child. In other words, I'm lucky my sister remembers to feed me.

He swears in Italian. "That's no life for you, Clara."

"And it's a life for you?"

"I would leave if I could," he says. "You know that."

"You turn eighteen in a year. Will you leave then?" My stomach clenches at the thought of him gone. I'm two years younger than him. And even when I turn eighteen, I won't be leaving. By then I'll be engaged to whoever my father picks for me.

Just like my sister. I shudder at the thought of her fiancé.

He shrugs. "We'll see."

I roll my eyes. I suspect he's making plans, but he isn't sharing them with me. That's how the men around here operate, keeping girls in the dark. Honor only found out she was engaged when Byron was invited over for dinner. He has the money and the power. She doesn't get a choice. Neither will I.

"If you go, you should take me with you," I say.

"I don't think Honor would appreciate me taking you away."

No, she wouldn't. And the thought of being without my sister makes my heart ache. Sometimes I give her a hard time, but I love her. I'd never leave her behind. "She can come with us. It will be like an adventure."

"Don't talk stupid, Clara." His eyes flash with anger and something else I can't define.

I jerk back, hurt. "It was just an idea."

"Well, it's a bad idea. Your father is never gonna let you leave."

Deep inside, I turn cold. I know that's true. Of course it is. Giovanni doesn't have the money or the resources to take us away from here. And even if he did, why would he want to?

I hate myself for even suggesting it. How desperate can I look?

Shaking inside, I stand up and grab the bottle of Jack Daniels. It's heavier than I would have expected, but I carry it over to a wet bar still stocked with decanters and wine glasses. No liquor though. There used to be huge parties here. When my mother died, they stopped.

We're supposed to have a party in a few days, though, to celebrate my sister's engagement. I'm not even allowed to go. I'll just be able to see the fireworks from the window.

Without a word Giovanni joins me, his heat both comforting and stark. He takes the glass from my shaking hand. He opens the bottle and pours the deep amber liquid inside. Then takes another cup for himself, twice as full.

"Why do you get more?" I protest, mostly because I like teasing him.

His expression is amused. "I'm bigger than you."

He is bigger. Taller and broader, though still skinny. His hands are bigger than mine too. They hold the glass with confidence, whereas I almost drop mine.

I take a sip before I can second-guess myself. "*Oh my God.*"

It burns my throat, battery acid scalding me all the way down.

His lips firm, like he's trying not to laugh. "Good stuff?"

"Oh, shut up." Then it doesn't matter because I'm laughing too. That stuff is *awful.*

He grins and takes a drink—more like a gulp. And he doesn't cough or wince after. "You get used to it."

"How much do I have to drink to get used to it?"

"More than you should."

I take another sip. It burns again, but I have to say, not as bad. It still doesn't taste good, but I'm determined to drink it anyway. This pool house is the only place where I can break the rules, where I can experience things. The pool house is the only place I even feel alive.

"Let's try mine," I say. My voice already sounds rougher from the alcohol.

He holds up the cigar. "Did you bring a lighter?"

"Oh, crap."

His eyes crinkle in that way I love. It makes my chest feel full, like there's no room for air. "It doesn't matter," he says.

"But I didn't hold up my end of the bargain."

He takes another drink. It looks so natural when he does it. "What bargain?"

"To do bad things," I say seriously. When your life is as controlled as mine, you need to plan these things. Tonight is supposed to be the night.

He looks down, a strange smile on his face. "Let's start with the whiskey. If that's not enough, we can knock over a bank or something."

I smack his arm. "You're making fun of me."

"Never." His eyes meet mine, and I see that he's not laughing at all. "I'd rob a bank if you wanted me to."

My stomach twists at his solemn tone. "I'd rather you stay safe," I whisper.

He reaches a hand toward me like he's going to cup my face, only half an inch away he freezes. I can almost feel the heat of him, and I remain very still, waiting to see what he'll do next.

He shoves his empty glass onto the bar and

walks away.

I let out a breath. What is that about? Lately we keep having these moments where it seems, like he's going to touch me. But he never does. I want to touch him too, but I don't. I wouldn't know where to start. I can't even imagine how he'd feel. Would he be like the whiskey, leaving a trail of fire? I'm scared to find out.

He's on the couch, so I join him there. Not touching, just sitting beside him.

"Gio, I'm worried about Honor."

He doesn't look at me. "She's strong. She can take care of herself."

"Yeah, but Byron is a jerk." And even she can't fight the tides. That's what men like Byron are. Tsunamis. Hurricanes. Natural disasters.

"Your dad wants someone who can take over. That's pretty much guaranteed to be an asshole."

He's not saying anything I don't know, but it's still frustrating. It's too dark to see his expression. I can only see the shape of him beside me, his neck and shoulders limned by moonlight. "This isn't the eighteenth century. This is Las Vegas."

"Marriage isn't about that. Not here."

It's about making alliances. It's about *money*. "He should make *you* the next one in line."

At least Gio has been around for years. His

dad is trusted here, even if he's not high ranking. This Byron guy hasn't even been in Las Vegas very long. And he's a cop. I learned from an early age not to trust cops—even dirty ones.

Gio shakes his head. "No, thanks."

"Why not? You'd be good at it." I can tell he's biting his tongue. "What?"

"Good at killing people?" he asks softly.

I flinch. Most of the time we skirt around what exactly my father does. And technically Gio is a part of that. I've never asked him if he's killed someone. For all I know, he already has robbed a bank. He's still in high school, so they're keeping him light. But once he graduates high school, they'll want to induct him. I'd almost rather he did leave then. Even though it would kill me to see him go.

He shakes his head. "Anyway, if it were me being groomed, I'd have to marry Honor. And I couldn't do that."

The thought of him marrying my sister makes my stomach knot. He's only a couple years younger than her. It's actually not a bad idea. "Why not?"

"Because I like her sister."

I go very still. There's only one sister. *Me.*

"What did you say?" I whisper.

"You heard me." He leans close. He reaches for me—and this time, his hand does cup my cheek. The feel of him is shocking, startling, impossibly coarse and warm at the same time. He runs his thumb along my skin, rasping against me. My eyes flutter closed.

The old leather of the couch creaks as he leans forward. He must be inches away now. His breath coasts over my lips. Goose bumps rise on my skin. I'm waiting...hoping...

Suddenly his lips are against mine, warm and soft. God, I've seen those lips smile and twist and curse a blue streak, but I never imagined they could be this soft. Nothing like whiskey, with its fire. This is a gentle heat, a caress, and I sink into him, let myself go lax.

One second later, he's gone. Not touching me at all.

My eyes snap open. "Gio?"

He looks tormented. I may not have felt the whiskey burn, but he did. Pain flashes through his eyes. He stands and walks away. "No, Clara. That was wrong. I was wrong to do that."

"But why?" How could that be wrong? That was the best thing that ever happened to me. On a night when I wanted to be *bad,* I experienced my first kiss. It's the best bad thing I could have imagined. And it tasted so sweet.

He's still shaking his head, so vehemently I'm not sure who he's trying to convince—me or himself. "You've been drinking."

"One drink," I say, kind of insulted. I may be new to this, but I'm not drunk.

"One drink is enough."

"You had one drink too," I point out, accusing.

He laughs, the sound unsteady and harsh. "I'm bigger than you."

I don't know if he means the drink affects him less or if it's just another reason why the kiss was a bad idea—as if he might have overpowered me. But there is no reason why this is a bad idea. I've wanted him to kiss me forever. And judging by the way he kissed just now, he liked it too. Unless…

My voice is small. "Did I…do it wrong?"

He lets out a string of curse words. "No, *bella*. You did nothing wrong. This is me. I can't touch you when you've been drinking. I can't touch you at all."

Want to read more? Tough Love is available on Amazon, iBooks, Barnes & Noble, Kobo, and other book retailers!

OTHER BOOKS
BY SKYE WARREN

Endgame series
The Pawn
The Knight
The Castle

Stripped series
Tough Love
Love the Way You Lie
Better When It Hurts
Even Better
Pretty When You Cry
Caught for Christmas
Hold You Against Me
To the Ends of the Earth

Chicago Underground series
Rough
Hard
Fierce
Wild
Dirty
Secret
Sweet
Deep

Criminals and Captives series
Prisoner

Standalone Dark Romance
Wanderlust
On the Way Home
His for Christmas
Hear Me
Take the Heat

Dark Nights series
Keep Me Safe
Trust in Me
Don't Let Go

The Beauty series
Beauty Touched the Beast
Beneath the Beauty
Broken Beauty
Beauty Becomes You
Loving the Beauty: A Beauty Epilogue

Visit skyewarren.com for the complete Skye
Warren book list, along with boxed sets,
audiobooks, and paperback listings.
Thank you for reading!

About the Author

Skye Warren is the New York Times bestselling author of contemporary romance such as the Chicago Underground and Stripped series. Her books have been featured in Jezebel, Buzzfeed, USA Today Happily Ever After, Glamour, and Elle Magazine. She makes her home in Texas with her loving family, two sweet dogs, and one evil cat.

Sign up for Skye's newsletter:
www.skyewarren.com/newsletter

Like Skye Warren on Facebook:
facebook.com/skyewarren

Join Skye Warren's Dark Room reader group:
skyewarren.com/darkroom

Follow Skye Warren on Instagram:
instagram.com/skyewarrenbooks

Visit Skye's website for her current booklist:
www.skyewarren.com

COPYRIGHT